Mississippi Comforts: True Stories of Redemption and Hope

Ray Flowers

To my good friends
Gene & Marilyn,
I gladly thank you
for your friendship.
In Christ,
Ray Flowers

ISBN: 1-4515-8183-1
ISBN-13: 9781451581836

Chapter 1
"Mrs. McClain's Happy School"
Age 5

The celebration of Labor Day on this Monday is finally here. The days are getting a little shorter. And the sun seems to go down faster now. The nights are cooler and Labor Day is a big deal. Mama fixes her famous ribs. She first boils these big pork ribs in cheap white wine. Last Saturday, she made her painter/helper Pat go into the "package" store to buy the wine. She would not be caught dead in a liquor store. But this recipe is time tested. She boils them on a high boil for an hour, and during that hour, I help her make the special BBQ sauce for them right before they hit the BBQ grill. As they are being carried out to the grill by my dad,..... my dog Fella perks up and gets interested in the unique smells. The ribs remain on the grill for about 15 minutes.

The feast begins shortly after noon. Mama's mustard potato salad is in the line up and I'm happy because she put out my portion before she added the pickles. Sweet pickles and I do not get along. One night last week, Daddy made a house call to someone I did not know. He told me they didn't have the money to pay him, but they gave him what they could. They had a big peach tree in their back yard. Daddy tells me while he was giving some sort of treatment to the woman, the husband told his 2 daughters to gather some bags of fresh peaches. That night Daddy brought home 5 grocery bags of fresh peaches. He tells me he gladly accepted those peaches for his payment.

Some of those peaches are in the home made ice cream being made. Thank goodness we have an electric ice cream maker because I hate those crank kind. Those are made for right handed people, and I don't qualify. My right arm gets tired. But that peach ice cream is worth having for breakfast, dinner, and supper. I guess that if I was stranded on a deserted island like "Gilligan's Island," my only request would be that peach ice cream was plentiful.

The day after Labor Day is the first day of school. As the sun goes down, my sisters start figuring out what they're going to wear, so I won't see them for hours. Tomorrow is my first day at school, too. I get to go to Mrs. McClain's Happy School. Some people call it Kindergarten, but I call it Mrs. McClain's Happy School. I can't wait.

In the distance, I hear Daddy fiddling with his short wave radio. It's black, and has lots of buttons on it, and a name spelled ZENITH. It also has a dial and Daddy's turning the dial. When I hear conversation, I join him in the den. I hear a language that's not mine. Daddy says he's listening to a radio station from a far away place called Germany. He knows how to speak that language and is listening closely.

He occasionally laughs and then moves the dial to pick up some other foreign place. Now he's listening to some place called——Scotland. I can understand a few of the words, but their accents are so strange, I don't understand how they communicate with each other. Daddy says we can only pick up these stations at night time. He says it's something about radio waves jumping. I guess I'll understand that someday, but not tonight.

Yesterday, mama took me to the store and bought me the list of things that Mrs. McClain asked I bring. We get a box of crayons, a 64 crayon box, with a built-in sharpener. Then we bought a few #2 pencils, and then, the big thing, my lunch box. I picked it out myself. "The Munsters" are a favorite TV show, so I got a lunch box with their pictures all over it. I am really proud of that. And Mama also bought a palate, but I don't know what I'm supposed to do with that.

Monday is here. I eat a big bowl of grits and butter with biscuits, and I'm ready to go. I grab all my stuff. I kissed my folks, and headed for the car. This car is a different piece of work. It is bright green and looks like a big matchbox with 4 doors. I get in the back seat. Nobody's there but me. I roll down the window and start yelling, "I'm in the car!" After what seems like an hour, my sisters come out and get in. Mama thinks my oldest sister Ruth is the most organized person on the planet. She says that because in the wintertime, Mama sends them to school each wearing a pair of gloves. Ruth always comes home with two gloves, and Maggie, my middle sister, only brings home one. "Maggie" is short for Mary Magdalene. Ruth has mapped out the entire route to Mrs. McClain's first, and then to Maggie's school, and then to her own. In most small towns, this kind of organization of routes is not necessary, but here it is vital, an element of survival. This car which Daddy bought for school use only makes left turns.

My sisters have learned to stop complaining to Daddy about that, because every time they do, he tells them they should be grateful it has 4 tires. That sometimes shuts them up, and sometimes not. One time my sisters tried to make a right turn, but the motor made a really scary noise and the horn started to blow non-stop, so they learned to get about town using only left turns. For sure it takes us longer to get somewhere, but we get there.

Mrs. McClain welcomes everyone individually, and calls each of us by our name, as if she already knew us and knew we were coming today. She smiles really big, and her face just lights up. Her smile reminds me of my grand-mama's smile, but Mrs. McClain has more teeth. Grandmama's hugs are bigger, and she always smells like turnip greens. Mrs. McClain, when she hugs, smells like chocolate cookies, and boy do I like cookies. Mrs. McClain's smile reminds me of something Mama told me during breakfast. She said, "Be nice today, because you don't know who's having a rough day, and maybe your smile is the only one they see today."

There are about 15 of us, and Jerry is friendly to me, and we kinda buddy-up. We instantly head for the merry-go-round. The others join us. We got that thing going round and round and faster and faster. Then I fall off. My body is on the ground, but my head has left planet Earth and is spinning out of control and is headed for orbit around the planet Pluto in deep space. I fight hard to keep my guts from exiting my body, especially my grits and biscuits.

Whew! That was FUN! Mrs. McClain calls us for book time. I walk crooked, out of control. I've seen only one other person walk like that. Pat, my Mama's helper/painter walks like that when we bail him out of jail for public drunkenness.

Onward to the slide. There are already 3 people in line so Jerry and I wait. I'm now at the top, and then push the bars so I can go faster. I go down slower than molasses in January. All this slide needs is some wax paper on my bottom. I'll bring that tomorrow.

Lunch time is great because everybody loves my lunch box. A new friend Angela likes it. That's a good sign. She's cute. Her hair is black and long, pulled into a pony tail.

Since we had graham crackers during book time, now it's fruit time. I am now experiencing a taste which distorts the contour of my face. It is SOOOOO far worse than bad. It is an unknown fruit from a different world. I would so gladly eaten something I hated, like pickled beets, to take the place of this horrible substance. Somebody called it a "grapefruit". I am so glad it has a name so I can stay far, far away. Even water doesn't get rid of the bad, bad taste, kinda like vomit.

Mrs. McClain begins to put all the palates on the floor. At first, I think the reason she's doing that is because of people passing out from eating those blasted grapefruits. But, no, they are being put out for SLEEP! Could it get any worse for me?

Sleeping is the last thing I want to do. I just laid there playing asleep. In reality, sometimes in sleep I have trouble holding in the contents of my bladder. And I really don't want to deal with that.....especially here.

Right after their school is out, my sisters Ruth and Maggie arrive to get me. Making only left turns, we head to a drive-in called "The Big R" out on Highway 45 to get a coke float. They visit with their friends for a while and leave me in the back seat, happy with my coke float.

Now we are headed for the house. I am excited about the next few days.

The next morning continues with the same left turns only route to Mrs. McClain's. It is now a proven successful route by "reliable Ruth."

I meet a new guy. He sez his name is "Jammy Jun." I say "Hello Jimmy John."He quickly corrects me. "I told you my name is Jammy Jun." I stand corrected. I then realize this young man is from the "stix." That's the term my family uses when we talk about somebody who lives way, way out in the county. I am learning that many people from Mississippi have double names. I can't figure that one out. Jammy Jun is nice to me, so we become friends. He is especially good at playing a game called "Red Rover." He is never lost to the other side. I always am. That fact alone puts him in a highly respected position.

Today is Tuesday and I am confused. There are conflicting smells coming from Mrs. McClain's kitchen. The first is a familiar smell of bleach, used for cleaning clothes. Willie Mae, Mama's helper, uses that nasty chemical at my house, too. The smell of peanut butter/chocolate cookies take over. I knew during book time they would be served and my ever-increasing sweet tooth would be quiet for a short time.

After book time, we learned about the value of having good manners. My Mama would absolutely have adored to be here to jump in helping Mrs. McClain pound that lesson in our heads. Thank God she's not here. We learn that manners are just that. The mannerisms we have and show toward others says a lot about who we are. She says manners don't judge us, they just tell others things about us without us saying a word. I didn't realize I was actually speaking a different language through my manners without me being aware of it. That is really interesting to me. I really don't understand why, but it's still really interesting.

Today, both Jerry and I brought wax paper for the slide. We both couldn't wait to try it. As soon as we are let outdoors, we head for the slide. Boy, does it work! We slide down that slide like greased lightning.

Suddenly, we are popular and everybody's asking if they can borrow the wax paper. We do, and the paper tears up the more it's used. But...no big deal.....we still have loads of fun.

During book time, my stomach starts to growl because I'm hungry. I look forward to the sausage sandwich Mama made me at breakfast. I am also looking forward to the special kind of potato chips I like, in addition to two cookies. I don't mention to tell Mama Mrs. McClain provides cookies every day. There are certain things I learn just by remaining silent. Cool.

Playing marbles on the playground is new to me. The playground is dirt. In most people's yard, there is grass, but not here. There are too many kids running around. This is a perfect place to play marbles. Jammy Jun explains what a "steelie" is. It is a larger marble than the others used for shooting at the smaller ones. We get a stick and draw a circle in the dirt and put the smaller marbles inside the circle. The goal is to shoot the smaller ones out of the circle.

Since this is new to me, I don't know which hand to use for shooting. First, I try with my left hand, and then when my next turn comes up, I try with my right hand. I find that either one works pretty well. That is weird because nobody else can do that. Am I weird or is everybody else? I get better the more we play.

Right before sleep time today, I now know the routine and go to the bathroom right before it, so no embarrassment for me today. I still don't like naps, but I can lay still for a few moments, pretending I am asleep.

Today we do something unusual. I learn my home telephone number and my address. I really don't understand why that might be valuable for me to know. I know who I am. I know where I live. Why should I memorize a bunch of numbers?

In the choosing of teams for Red Rover, I find myself tapping my foot, waiting to be chosen. I guess I don't like being left out. No, now that I think about it, I <u>KNOW</u> I don't like being left out.

Ruth and Maggie again pick me up on time. Ruth had to go to the drugstore before we make our trek to the "Big R", so again we use only left turns to get there. I guess Ruth has done this before so much she's memorized a few routes. She's not long in the drug store, so we head for the drive in. Today I break my routine and get a chocolate sundae instead of a coke float. This is really fine, even with a cherry on the top. During their visit with their friends, I finish my sundae. I am now bored and fidgety. I get out of the car and walk to join them. When they see me coming, they quickly say goodbye to their friends and say to me that's it's time to go. We now head for the house. I guess I learned something else today. Now I know how to make them hurry up. I like that.

Life is good at Mrs. McClain's Happy School.

###Author's comments; 1) an occasional feast is a good thing, 2) a very unusual car is a good thing, 3) the ability to manufacture fun is a life lesson.

Chapter 2
"Yes, my Mother has, does now, and will continue to control me from the Choir Loft"
Age 12

Some things are predictable, and others which ought to be predictable are totally irrational. Take, for instance, my faithful dog Fella. He is very predictable. He is always glad to see me, glad to be with me, and glad to participate in whatever activity comes to my mind that day. On the other hand, take my evil older sister. She is totally unpredictable and totally irrational. One moment, I am the best little brother who ever lived, and 3.5 minutes later she's so angry at me she's telling me a detailed story of how I am not really a member of the family, that I was adopted, and Mama and Daddy speak often about taking me back to the orphanage, if they'll take me.

There is one thing which is very predictable at my house, and it's what goes on around my house on Sunday mornings. Mama is the choir director at my Methodist Church, so she has certain responsibilities. She usually gets up before everybody else in the family, and starts cooking. Sunday "Dinner" (noon time) is a big deal at my house. She usually prepares the Sunday dinner meal before she starts getting ready to take the family to church. Today she is "fixing" a casserole, with rice at the bottom, and then chicken breasts scattered around, and mushroom soup is poured over the top and allowed to work its way down. It's one of my favorites. I really like it when she puts almonds or pecans scattered on the top. She then puts a top on it and cooks it slowly in the oven on a low temperature while we are away at church. And the smells when we open the side door after church WOW! Today our "green" is English peas. She, for some untold reason, won't buy green peas. She wants small English peas. Go figure.

By 8 or so, I'm up and sitting in front of the TV watching the 3 Stooges. Curly, Moe, and Larry are their names. I am watching the 3 Stooges today because mama laughed when I was watching Bugs Bunny yesterday on Saturday morning cartoons. I was watching the hunter Elmer Fudd hunt for Bugs Bunny, singing "Kill the Wabbit!" "Kill the Wabbit!" That's when she started laughing. She says to me, "I did not know you liked Classical Music." I said I didn't. She informed me the background music for that scene is a famous song called "Flight of the Valkyries". I wanted nothing to do with Classical Music, so today I am watching the 3 Stooges, and really laughing.

Evidently, I was laughing so hard I drew her attention in the kitchen, not too far away. She takes the opportunity to ask me to go out to the clothes line and get some towels and washcloths. So, in the next commercial break, I go out the back door, go around the house where the clothesline is, and start retrieving the requested items. I notice some sheets were hanging there as well. There is an unmistakable smell about clothes, especially bed sheets, when they are allowed to dry on the clothesline. It's a fresh, clean smell. I faintly smell the nearby pines in them. I grab the sheets, and put them right in front of my nose and smell a very familiar smell. Then I go back to the house with the towels and washcloths.

Now, I'm back in front of the TV. Daddy walks by, says "Hey boy", and rubs my head as I sit on the floor. He's headed for the hospital, to make "rounds", meaning to check on all his patients in the hospital. That will take a while, and he will meet us at church later.

And I then again think about the irrational thought of giving me a name. Nobody ever uses it.

About 8:15, I go and take a shower, and for a good reason. I make a point to take a shower before either of my sisters, because both of them each use all the hot water that poor hot water tank can put out. I'm not into cold showers. Then I am dressed and ready for breakfast. Sunday morning is a "do it yourself" deal for breakfast. So, I dig in the freezer, and find some frozen waffles. I put 2 of them in the toaster, and pour some Aunt Jamima maple syrup and them and I'm back at the TV. After I'm done, I take my plate out to Fella and let him enjoy the syrup.

Sunday School starts at 9:30, so we have to leave the house about 9:25. It's a 4 minute ride. Mama deposits me in class with Mrs. Fulgham. She is so mean; she makes us listen to some story on the record player. Then we sing a hymn from the Cokesbury hymnal and listen to all the wrong notes she hits. It is so boring. After the record ends, she then asks us questions about the subject on the player. I can't wait to get out of here. I think I'd rather be at the dentist getting my braces adjusted. Then, we hear feet rustling from next door and know its 10:30, time to leave. She says a prayer, and we bolt.

While I am at Sunday School, mama is in the rehearsal room with the choir with last minute touch ups to the upcoming two anthems. I hang around in the corner. Miss Cottrell always has Juicy Fruit gum for me, and signals for me to come and get a piece. Mama then signals me to go on to the sanctuary. I then run at a fast walk pace toward the fellowship hall. That's where the coke machine is. I put in a dime and get my Sprite and head straight outside to visit with my friends. I see my friend Harry, who is a little older and works for his dad in their family furniture store. I ask him if he's staying busy, and he says, "Ray, the only spare time I have is between Sunday School and Church." I thought that was funny. He's a good guy. I also see a friend of my eldest sister. His name is Kenny. He is tall, played college football, and leans down and shakes my hand. Then he tells me he's been thinking about running for mayor of

West Point. Then he asks me my opinion. I say I think it's a great idea. I think he's already made up his mind to run, but was just letting me know he was running so I would tell my parents when we got home.

It's about 5 minutes before the service, so I walk in, and am handed a bulletin. I see the big sanctuary, with maroon carpet, and beautiful stained glass windows, 3 big ones on each side. They are pictures of the disciples, either fishing, or whatever. And there is a huge stained glass window in the street side of the sanctuary, or behind the pulpit. In between the pipes to the pipe organ is a picture of Jesus and the little children, and some scripture under it. But I know where I'm going. I am to sit on the 3rd row from the front, 3 adult seats inward. Nobody but me sits in that area, so I usually have to guess at it, but I always get it right.

Then the organist starts playing the start the worship hymn, and everybody stands, turns their hymnals to number 273, and the choir marches in from the back, down the center aisle.

Familiar faces pass by me and smile, and at last, Pastor Johnny Dinas passes me and goes out of his way to quickly come shake my hand. I like him. He then goes into the pulpit. After the song, everybody is seated and Brother Dinas takes over. Little does he know that there is a lot of shifting and maneuvering going on with me and my mother. She has her special spot in the alto section of the choir and I am expected to shift myself to the exact position. And that position is where she can see my every move. She has a straight shot view of me. It's better than what I could do with my rifle, and I am good. I know just how much fidgeting and shifting and slouching I can do. I speak with authority in these matters. I know my limits. I know her limits. Her looks at me with either a look signaling "it's OK," or there is a look similar to that of a mama alligator about to eat one of its own. I have tested those limits too far only one time. One time I slid over toward the center where she could not see me at all because of the floral arrangement. I was sitting with my friend Dave, and we were playing cards on the pew. Right after the last anthem and as Brother Dinas began his sermon, my mother raised herself up, got out of the choir loft, and as she marched over to me with a foul look on her face and with a death stare with those piercing deep brown eyes, I knew I was toast. Everybody was staring, and some were giggling. I was so embarrassed. But I knew the worse part was yet to come. After we got home, she took me into the playroom and said the infamous words; "I am disappointed in you." That did it. I'm crushed. So I learned my lesson well.

But today, I think about that most embarrassing day briefly, and then move on. I am thinking about what I am going to do this afternoon.

It's about 11:20, time for Brother Dinas to begin his sermon. I hear a familiar sound in the back. The door opens, and in comes my Daddy with a wooden caned back chair he got from the classroom next door.

He sits in the chair, and then leans back in the chair, so that it's on two legs, and he's leaned upon the back wall.

After the sermon, something unusual happened. Brother Dinas got away from the pulpit and came down at the floor level. He said: "I want to close today with a story my mother told me as a child. (I perked up and listened). There was a very poor woman, a beggar, who was homeless and stayed close to the river, because there was a lot of foot traffic along the river. As the woman is walking a familiar path, over in the bushes, she spots something very unusual. She walks over to it and finds a shiny stone. This is a brilliant stone, and she knows this is not just any stone; this is a very valuable stone. She knew her money troubles were over. She knew she was now wealthy. She smiled, looked at the stone with great admiration, and then put it in her bag. All her needs were over, she thought. She then continues her walk, dreaming about the new found riches. Along her way, a poor man, whom she did not know, comes up to her and asked her for something to eat, for he had not eaten in two days. She said, 'Of course.'" She dropped to her knees, opened the bag, and drew out a loaf of bread, which she broke, and gave some to him. With the bag still open, the man saw the brilliant stone, the one she had just found. He asked, "That stone, it's beautiful, may I have it, please?" She said, "Of course," and gave it to him and they parted. That man knew it was very valuable and his money problems were over. He was rich. That night, he could not sleep. He was troubled, but could not figure out why. As he lay awake, he then knew what was troubling him. The next day he searched for that woman he encountered yesterday, and after a few hours of searching, he found her. He said to her; "Here. Take this stone. It belongs to you. I can't keep it. But I do know what I want from you. I want something far, far more valuable than that stone." She thought to herself, "I have nothing, I have absolutely nothing". He then said; "I want whatever it is inside you that made you so willing to give that stone to me."

Then Brother Dinas closed the service with a blessing.

I really hope I never forget that story.

I walk to the back of the sanctuary, join my Daddy, and we head home.

####Author's present day comments: 1) dealing with difficult people, 2) the art of getting along with people you don't like, 3)recognition of consequences of my behavior, 4) being dependable, 5)comedy.

Chapter 3
Age 12, Fall 1965
'THE REAL SOUND
OF MUSIC'

Why does the season after Summer have two names, Fall and Autumn? I've wondered that before. Even Mama and Daddy admit they don' know, so I assume nobody else knows either. They know just about everything.

School has started. My prayers have been answered. Mama has given up on making me wear Engineer Boots and not letting me wear blue jeans. Wow, what a victory that is. Tennis shoes and jeans are what I wear now.

I still have a pair of jeans I wore on the 4th of July. That was a big day of home-made ice cream and firecrackers on the patio. During a Roman Candle war, I wasn't quite fast enough to miss one of the fireballs my friend Mike Murphree shot at me. It hit my knee and burned a hole in my jeans. Now they look really cool. I was able to dodge all the shots from Dave Riley and Robert McGlohn. They are really not very good shots.

Last Friday, before school, the 4 of us took our last ride on the train that goes through town. We have a cool system. We know the times the train comes through town. So we park our bikes in some bushes and give ourselves time to walk across town to catch the train as it slows way down as it passes through town. After covering ourselves in the bushes, we wait for just the right kind of train car to hop onto. We spotted one coming and started to run. The easy part is hopping on. It's a fun ride, just a little bumpy. As the engineer passes through town and is on the other side, we feel him start to speed up, and that's our signal to look for an opportunity to jump off. We learned the exit part the hard way. When we first did this we'd jump and just fall down. Not cool. It took us a few times to learn how to jump and then roll to make the exit much smoother. Most of the time, we would land not to far from our hidden bikes, and the last time was no exception. Then we doubled up on our bikes to go get the ones we started out on.

It was a good Summer.

Mrs. Busby is my teacher since there is only one 6th grade class. She is new, so nobody knows anything about her. She puts us in seats where she could call on us by our names. Lucky for me, I am seated toward the back, sitting by Beth, and Angela, and Beverly. Not bad, not bad at all.

As the first few weeks go by, it's harder and harder for me to see what she is writing on the blackboard. Is she writing so small? It seems fuzzy, and I ask so many questions, she moves me to the front row. Not cool, but I can see. Now I am sitting by the twins, Dennis and Stennis Oliver.

Little did I know that Mrs. Busby had called Mama and told her she thought my eyes should be checked. Next thing I know I'm wearing glasses. I look goofy. Robert McGlohn's glasses are as thick as the bottom of a bottle of Coke. Now we have even more in common. He is now known as Mr. McGoo #1, and I am known as Mr. McGoo #2. I don't know if that's a good thing or a bad thing, it just is what it is. Anyway, I see much better, it just took a couple of weeks to get used to them.

There was a little piece of bad luck while I was getting used to them. While I was mowing the grass in our yard, they fall off by accident. The really bad part was that I ran over a frog at the same time. I can't forget seeing parts of my glasses and parts of the frog coming out of the side. It was a real mess. Mama and Daddy understood, and so it wasn't long before I had a new pair, and those fit more tight on my head.

One really good signal that Fall is here is that My Mama starts chopping on things outside. There is usually a full, beautiful Mimosa tree right outside my bedroom window. But no more. That poor thing is chopped down to just a nub. She calls it "pruning." I call it "butchering."

Every time she does that if reminds me of something my Daddy says; "Don't cut down a tree in Winter." Pop, my Daddy's Dad, told him of a young man needing firewood to stay warm. He cut down what he thought was a dead apple tree. In the Spring, the family had everything they needed, except apples. Actually, it looked dead. The limbs cracked. But is wasn't dead at all, it was just dormant in Winter waiting for Spring. Daddy says it's the same about people. He says, "Don't criticize a person down on their luck." I have not forgotten that.

We get the Memphis newspaper, The Commercial Appeal, every Sunday. Last Sunday, after church, I saw that Mama was looking for something special, I just didn't know what. Since it's a big paper, thick as the Sears and Roebuck catalog, it took her a while, but she finally found what she was looking for. She was looking for, and found, a new movie that had just come out, called, "The Sound of Music." That crazy woman jumped around the den like a monkey on a pogo stick. I felt like it was Christmas morning! She quickly found a calendar and began looking for a day when the family could go see this movie. It didn't take her long to find a date. Then she TOLD Daddy he was taking off that Friday, go to Memphis, and we would return late Saturday night. That's the first time I have ever heard Mama TELL Burnell Flowers ANYTHING, except telling him to stay out of her kitchen. That kitchen is sacred territory.

Daddy had a bewildered look on his face, kinda like a deer in headlights. And then he used extremely good judgment, and said, "Sounds good to me."

That sounded pretty good to me, too. At least, in Memphis, at the very least, we won't get a telephone call for him and for to him ask them, "What color is the mucus?" while we are eating.

Mama's plan quickly goes into action. In two weeks, we, meaning me, Mama, Daddy, and Maggie will travel. Ruth has married a really good guy named David. They live in New Orleans where he is in medical school. New Orleans is really a fun place.

We will travel to Oxford on Friday. Mama and Daddy lived there when Daddy just got out of medical school. Later in the day, we will travel a little while on the Natchez Trace and end up in Memphis for the night.

Today is Thursday, and everybody, is excited to go. We will be traveling in what everybody knows is "Mama's car", a Buick Electra 225. During the day today, Mama has packed for herself, Daddy and me! Maggie is so picky, so Mama lets her do her own packing. We eat a light Supper, 'cause we have a full two days ahead of us.

My wind-up alarm clock starts its horrible sound at 7. Everybody else is already up, and Mama is in the kitchen fixin grits, biscuits, and sausage. She has sausage now since it's past Labor Day. We'll go back to bacon after Easter. Why does she do that? God only knows, but I have heard her say, "It's cold enough to kill hogs." Doesn't make any sense to me, but who am I? I'm only 12. From where I am in the playroom, I hear Daddy ask Mama if they need to get gas. She tells him she got it filled up and serviced at

Carother's Service Station yesterday after she had taken Willie Mae home.

We leave around 8. Maggie and I are in the back seat as far apart from each other as possible. Daddy is driving, and as we leave town and get more in the country, the leaves are already turning on some of the trees. I am not used to seeing all this color so close, because we have 96 pine trees on our place, and they stay green all the time. We pass Cedar Bluff, and right after that, we get on The Natchez Trace. Daddy explains that the Natchez Indians made a trade route that starts at the coast of Natchez, near the end of the Mississippi River. He says it goes all the way up through Mississippi, into Tennessee, and ends at Nashville, Tennessee.

We stay on the Trace for a while and get off near Tupelo. Daddy makes a point to go through Tupelo to show us where Elvis Presley was born and raised.

That little wooden house is so small, I KNOW I could easily throw a baseball in the front door and it come out the back door and then roll some more.

Mama sez that if Elvis would just stay still and learn to pronounce his words, she'd like him more. She also says he has ants in his pants. Maggie laughs and tells Mama that him wiggling his hips while he sings is what people like. Daddy just shakes his head and sez, "You can take the boy of the country, but you can't take the country out of the boy."

Pontotoc is the next town. I learned about Chief Pontotoc in Miss. History class. He tried really hard to make peace with the people moving in. Our next stop is Oxford. Daddy is paying close attention. He went to school here at a college called "Ole Miss." He sez their mascot is, "The Rebels." He talks about their famous football team. He then remembers a saying they had, "We may not win every game, but ain't never lost a party." We all laugh. As Daddy is driving through the town, he sez, "It has changed so much." Mama chuckles and says, "The only constant in life is change." I don't get the joke. Daddy turns to many places, wanting to see familiar sights. They show Maggie and me the house they lived in while they were here. They drive by several houses, and say, "So and so lived here", and then a then across the street they say, "So and so lived there." This is a small town. It looks smaller than West Point.

We drive around a corner and Mama sez, "That's where Billy lived." She then sez, "Billy Faulkner, but his readers know him as William Faulkner." She continues, "He's a writer of books, and we knew him because we had some common friends, and I knew him better than Daddy because he dated my sister Corrine for awhile, but she broke up with him." Daddy sez, "In 1949, Faulkner won a Nobel Prize for Literature." I asked him, "What's a 'no bell'?" All three of them just shake their heads. I still don't get it. I musta said somethin stupid. Daddy sez, "I started my medical practice here with a great Doctor named "Dr. Billy Guyton." Daddy also sez, "He became a mentor of mine." I see a small tear coming from Daddy's eyes as he stopped the car in front of The Guyton Clinic. Daddy then said,

"Dr. Guyton and I worked closely together for 2 years, and Dr Guyton had many children. I thought all of them would be Doctors because their Daddy was so brilliant." Daddy continues, "When Dr. Guyton found out that the leaders in West Point wanted me and Harvey to move to West Point and name the hospital, 'Flowers Hospital,' he came into my office and shut the door. He then said to me, 'Burnell, you have 2 golden doors right in your face. You know you are welcome to stay here and practice, or go to West Point with your brother Harvey and do grand things. Burnell, there are no wrong choices here. God Almighty has His hand in both of them----God is interested in you pleasing Him, but He's also interested in what goes on in that deep, deep, dreaming heart of yours.'" Dr Guyton continued, "Burnell, go back, way back to when you were that dreamy child......let that dreamy child make this decision for you, and it will be the right one."

There was a dead silence in the car. There was humility in that car. There was God Himself in that car. Thus, an era began in that moment of his decision.

Mama breaks the silence with, "We're finished here, so let's all take a bathroom break and get a Coke." Everyone agrees.

After the break, Maggie and I climb into the back seat. Maggie suggests we have a burping contest. I am an easy sucker to enter a burping contest. I can put out some weird sounds, but Maggie is the undisputed leader. She can produce some burps that pale the sound of a bassoon, but the

funniest part is the expressions on her face. She wins.....
hands down. She had a burp that lasts a whole 40 seconds.
Mama and Daddy are laughing their heads off.

It was a little surprise to me at how little time it takes
us to get to Memphis. Mama and Daddy seem to know
where they are going. That's comforting, and is a good thing,
b' cause I know my Daddy wouldn't stop and ask directions.
We would be forced to sleep in the car for untold days
before he would lower himself to do such a thing as that.

We turn into the parking lot of a hotel. Mama tells us
it's a nice hotel, and that there will be a surprise for us. I like
surprises. I can deal with that.

We get checked into the Hotel and we decided earlier
that we would just clean up and eat Supper at the Hotel. I
don't know why we have to clean up. We've just been riding. The meal is really good. I had the catfish fried in peanut
oil. I love that. And I substituted my fries for an extra dose
of those hush-puppies. After all that, I still have a little room
for dessert. I get vanilla ice cream, with crushed Oreo s,
and a few Strawberries. To my surprise, they put whipped
cream on top! Wow! Could it get any better? As I cut into
my first bite, a typical response comes without any sort of
surprise. Mama sez, "Let me have just a bite of that." What
can I say? What can I do? I give her my fork and she gets
the biggest bite that could fit into her mouth! I say nothing
I, simply, was in dreamland eating what little she left. That
was really fine. I don't like to think about fried catfish and

Ice cream mixing it all up in my stomach, but that's not my department.

We get up and walk toward the elevator and go to the 4th floor. Daddy opens the door we see 2 double beds!. Yuk! That means I have to sleep with Maggie. She ALWAYS steals the covers. And every time we sleep together I roll over onto a prickly hair roller that's fallen out. Her stealing the covers leaves me with icicles hanging from my nose. Daddy likes to sleep with the room really cold. We all know how adapt. Mama sets the clock to make us up at 7. Daddy reads one of those mystery Mickey Spillane books as the rest of us fall asleep.

WOW! That alarm clock is loud! We all get our showers and we don't run out of hot water! What a relief. At home, I feel sorry for that gas water heater because of Maggie. We get dressed and are in the restaurant by 8: 15. Mama looks all about seemingly like she knows something.

The waiter takes our order. I get waffles. They're big and round, not like those square ones we have at home. They gave me pure maple syrup, close to that Aunt Jimama that Mama buys, but this syrup is heated up and melts the butter on my waffles. Think Willie Mae can do all this?

Daddy keeps looking at his watch. Something is cooking, but I don't have a clue.

At 10 minutes until 9, Daddy gets up and sez, "Let's go now, just follow me." We march toward the elevators, but Daddy pushes no buttons. He sez, "Just wait here."

So here I am, waiting for the Earth to move. In a couple of moments, I see something really, really odd. An elevator door opens and the elevator man holds the doors open so that 12 ducks march single-file. They march and quack, then quack and march straight through the lobby for all to see. This is really weird, but I love it! They march to their small fountain of water and seem to be happy. Daddy sez they will stay there until 3, when they will march back across to the same elevator and go somewhere upstairs.

That was really fun. But I have to admit it. My trigger finger did twitch a bit, and I did think about my shotgun.

The movie starts at 11, so we get a move on. It takes us about 10 minutes on foot to get to the movie theater. There is already a line for purchasing tickets. Daddy tells me to rush ahead and get into the line. Shortly, they join me. We walk inside and head straight for the smells.....the popcorn at the concession stand. With a family sized bucket of popcorn and get some cokes. We find some good seats and we are set.

At first, the screen lights up with 2 cartoons. I ashamed to say I have not seen either of them.

For the next 2 1/2 hours, we all experience the escape of the Von Trapp family in a "musical." I have never seen anything like this before. Mama just keeps repeating, while whispering, "The music, the music." It is beautiful. During those 1 1/2 hours I have to go to the bathroom only once. Maggie grumbles as she take me up the stairs of the dark theater. We're back in a flash.

This experience is like a really cool dream. I feel like I am with them singing, dancing, and running for their lives.

When the movie is over, all the people start clapping, and smiling, and it seems to last a really long time. As we walk up the stairs to the lobby, all 4 of us are humming our favorite songs. Daddy was humming the Captain Von Trapp song. Mama was humming "The Impossible Dream." Maggie was singing, "I am six-teen, you are seven-teen".....and I was humming, "Good night, good night, good night."

While we are in the lobby, we find them selling 33 1/3 albums of the sound track of the movie. Mama gets that "I've got to buy those shoes" look in her eyes and she orders Daddy to go buy the album. Using his wisdom, he does so.

I think he would climb a mountain if she asked him to.

Now it's about 1:30. I thought we'd head back to West Point. No no. Mama and Daddy are sneaky. Daddy drives for a little while and just as I see the head of a giraffe, Mama sez, "We're headed for the Memphis Zoo!" Maggie and I are a' hootin and a' hollerin in the back seat. This is way too cool.

As we park at the zoo, I can hear the animals "doin their thing" in the distance. Daddy puts on a really silly looking hat because he's fair skinned. It's embarrassing, but I can deal with it.

After we get the red and white tickets, we walk through the turn stiles, Daddy stops all of us for a moment. He sez, "If we get separated or just get lost, just ask someone to point to this stature of Elvis at 5." Then, he sez, "Boys go this way and girls go that way." Daddy and I head straight for the reptiles. I see all kinds of snakes, some colorful, and some not at all. I also see alligators, crocodiles, and huge turtles. Those alligators are so big I bet one of them eating me would just be a snack. But I bet Tarzan could wrestle with one of them.

Next, we head for giant cats, the lions and tigers. Those lions are huge! And they are so beautiful, until they open the mouth......fangs. Reminds me kinda of like what Maggie looks like in the mornings. These lions are really big. I think shooting them with my .22 rifle would just make them mad. As we walk past them, Daddy sez, "The female, the mama, does all the killing." I don't get it. I ask Daddy, "So why is HE called the 'King of the Jungle?'"Daddy just laughs and shakes his head. The tigers are the most beautiful. Daddy says they're pretty sneaky, too. I can understand why after he tells me they sometimes hang out in trees, just waiting......

The giraffes are close, so we walk toward them. They're necks are SO long! And their legs are kinda skinny.

They have spots of different colors. They can get the fruit from the tall trees.

The camels are right next to the giraffes. We wander in that direction. These camels are taller than I expected. They've got a really funny-looking face. I've seen some people like that. Their fur looks really smooth. All of them are the same color and the same height. How do the owners tell them apart from each other? Maybe their teeth are different. Daddy tells me not to make one of them angry, because they spit. That's some advice I will take seriously. We sure don't have animals like this back home, and I think I am really glad.

The monkey cages are next. They are really loud. They all have a different kind of scream. And the cage where the chimps are has a trainer in there with them, playing with them. When he asks one of the chimps, "Do you want a banana?" The chimp then nods his head up and down, screaming, as if to say, "Yes, you idiot!"

The gorilla cages are our last stop before we go and meet up with Mama and Maggie. There are 4 gorillas. Three of them are moving around on the make-believe mountain. One of them remains motionless. I can barely see him breathing. He seems to be staring at me. Isn't it supposed to be the other way around? He must find me funny-looking. And I could say the same thing about him. Daddy's been chomping on a bag of roasted peanuts.

I have an idea. I dig into Daddy's bag and find the biggest one.

Baseball is my game back home. But I am NO pitcher! I can throw out a 3rd base runner toward home from right field. I'm good at that. But, again, I say, I am NO pitcher. I just happen to have a strong arm.

I am determined to make this gorilla move! And I change my mind. I grab a few more from Daddy's bag.

The first throw lands one near his feet. He is not impressed and remains motionless. Two more tries get the same result.

Daddy's getting a big kick out of this while I decide to take a more drastic measure. I grab the biggest peanut, the one I had held back. I place it in my right hand. I do a wind-up just like Whitey Ford or Sandy Kaufax do on TV. I throw that peanut hard as I can aiming for his face. That peanut is now traveling at light speed headed straight for his mouth! I see that gorilla open his mouth for 2 seconds while the peanut rolls right into his mouth! His head never moves! I turn to Daddy with my mouth hanging to the cement.. Daddy's laughing while I am in shock. I have NEVER been that accurate in my life! BUT I DID MAKE HIM MOVE! Daddy and I just stood there laughing. Daddy sez, "He kinda looks like Buddha." I ask, "Bubba who?"
He shakes his head and sez, "Never mind."

Daddy sez, "It's time to move back toward the starting point, the statue of Elvis." We stand there for a few minutes, just soaking up all the scenery. Daddy turns one direction and then turns the opposite way very quickly, lowering his head laughing. I ask him, "What's wrong?"He sez, "Nuthin, I just saw something I have never seen before." I ask, "What?" He sez, "You see that man and women over there, flaling their hands, arms, legs and feet?" I look that direction and notice they're not speaking. Daddy sez, "That's two mutes arguing, and they're not making a sound!" Now, I get it and we stand there laughing. I have never seen an argument like this one before, either. The funny thing for me is that I don't have a clue what they were saying to each other, but I know it wasn't nice.

As we gather ourselves, I ask Daddy a question, "How can you tell who won the argument?"

He slowly thinks about that question, and sez, "The one left standing, I guess." Sounds good to me.

We meet up with Mama and Maggie and begin our trek home. We swap stories all the way home. Their stories aren't nearly as interesting as ours.

I have had a really fun couple of days.......really fun.

####Author's present day comments: 1) Organization, 2)the art of listening, 3) living in the state of expectancy, 4) anticipation of planned upcoming events,
    5) When it's time for the leader to "back off", 6)Comedy.

Chapter 4
Age 12, 1966
"The Year Granddaddy Died"

It's late Summertime, and lots of stuff is going on. Labor Day is coming up, and so is school. Our, neighbor, Miss Roth, has 3 giant pecan trees in her back yard. Mama says her type of pecan trees give out pecans every other year. This must be one of those years, because my arm muscles are sore from the buckets of pecans I have been picking up for days. And my hands are sore from cracking all those pecans and pulling out the nut. Even my eyes are tired. I eat the ones I pull our whole, and that's just a few.

Mama's been making lots of pecan pies in these past few days. After they cool down from the oven, she covers them with foil and puts them in the big deep freezer out back.

That's not really a good sign. All of us know when somebody we know dies, Mama takes the family a pecan pie. There must be 12 to 14 pies in that freezer by now. I hope she's not planning on 12 or 13 people dying this winter, but if they do, she's got it covered.

This morning she told me we were going to Starkville, a nearby town. She didn't say why. Sometimes she tells me, sometimes not.

Dinner is great, as usual. Willie Mae has meat loaf, smashed potatoes, and butter beans, (I call them blowta-beans, 'cause they make me blow up). Whatever she does to that meat loaf is magical. Daddy especially likes her butter beans, so Willie Mae automatically knows to bring to the table his pepper sauce to put on those beans. It's a small rectangular glass bottle filled with tiny peppers of all different colors, then it's filled with white vinegar. It has a cork for a top, and he takes that cork off and drowns those beans with all that hot sauce. He does that with all green vegetables. When the bottle gets low, she simply adds more and more vinegar. Those peppers have been in there for as long as I can remember. Maybe they have been in there since before I was born.

When it's time to take Willie Mae home, I ride along because she intends to go to Starkville from there. I guess I'm along just for my good looks. I don't seem to have a purpose on this trip. She tells me she needs a new pair of shoes from Bauche's Department Store. I would add one minor correction to that. She WANTS a new pair of shoes. She already has more than anybody in the family. Her weakness is shoes is kinda like my weakness for chocolate, I guess. Bauche's Store is the place where she used to take me to get those awful Engineer Boots she made me wear to school when I was little. I don't think I will ever forget how uncomfortable those things were. And on top of that, she took get pride in shining those awful black boots every night. There had to be some evil to all that, I just don't know where.

As she's shopping in the store, I am walking the sidewalks of Starkville. I see many college students around town because this is the place where Mississippi State University is. In sports, we root for Mississippi State University. But when they play Ole Miss, Daddy gets out a coin and says, "Heads, Ole Miss., tails MSU." That way, he wins so matter who wins, 'cause he went to both schools. The same thing happens when MSU plays The University of Southern Mississippi, because that's where Mama got her music degree. She flips a coin, and roots for the one who lands heads up, 'cause she didn't attend both, just Southern.

What seems about 3 hours later, Mama needs my help with loading her new treasures into the car. Now, I have found my purpose.

She had parked the car in a metered space. When I saw her put a bunch of coins in the meter, I should have figured it out. But sometimes I'm a little slow.

Now she's headed into the University campus. Heehee, I know now we're headed for the bakery. They are famous for what miracles they produce in that bakery. The smells as we enter the bakery put me under a spell of some kind. I smell chocolate, caramel, coconut, and there are just some smells I can't figure out. I could stay in here for days.

As she looks through the glass to see all the baked goods on display, I am closely watching. I like to predict and guess which ones she will buy. Today, I'm guessing Coconut Cake and Chess Pie.

Darn! I'm only half right. She gets a Chess Pie and a Chocolate Cake. But who's complaining? For sure, it's not me! We love the stuff from the bakery and she heads back toward West Point.

She takes the short cut, and goes by the big turkey farm. It belongs to my friend Paul's uncle Pete. He has so many uncles, I can't get them all straight. There seems to be millions of turkeys, just hanging out. Some are much bigger than the others. Paul tells me that his uncle has to put the turkeys under a shed when it rains. When I asked, "Why so?" He told me, "They are so stupid, if they look up when it's raining, the rain will go into their noses and they will drown." I haven't really seen that happen, and I have my doubts about what Paul said. I know they're stupid, but they can't be THAT stupid! It just don't make sense.

Not far from the turkey farm on U.S. 45, there's a Choctaw Indian Burial Ground. There's a big sign there put by the government saying that's a special place. That's where the Indians buried their dead. They dug a big round and deep hole, and would bury people in it when they died, and then cover them up, waiting for the next layer. Seems a little odd to me, but hey, it worked for them until we ran them off.

Mama stops at the Mound. This is very unusual. She just says, "Come on, boy." Now, she's beginning to sound like Daddy. She must have something on her mind. She tells me, "There's some really good things behind that Mound." I ask, "Like what?' She says, "You'll see soon enough."

She opens the trunk of the car. I see two pair of work gloves, a bucket, and a small shovel. She tells me, "Put on these gloves." I do so. I ask her, "You gonna dig up some worms for my fishin?"

"No, Silly, we're going to pick some wild berries", she says. Sounds good to me. Willie Mae can do some mighty fine stuff making cobblers.

We walk behind the Indian Mound, and find a huge patch of all kinds of berries. There are blackberries, blueberries, and strawberries, and some I can't figure out. I ask her, "What's the shovel for?" She says, "Snakes." My antennas go straight up and I move closer to her. I am surprised this "lady" is doing this. This isn't like her. I ask her, "Why didn't you get Willie Mae or Pat to do this for you?"

She says, "I used to do this at my home town, Kilmichael, when I was your age, and I like to remember that." All this sounds a little weird to me, but I'm easy.

It takes about a half hour to fill our bucket. When she sees it's full, she says, "Take the bucket and the shovel to the car." Now I know my other purpose of the day. We throw the dirty gloves in the truck and then head for home.

After Supper, the phone rings, and naturally, Daddy answers it, assuming it's the Hospital calling for him. I hear him say, "Hello Sister!" He doesn't have a sister, so now I know it's Mama's older sister, Corrine, who lives in their home town, Kilmichael. There are four of the girls, all having nicknames. "Sister", has a real name, Corrine. "Eelii", the youngest has a name. Her name is Ellen. "Pretty Baby" is really Frances. "Boolie", is my mother, Beulah.

Daddy now has a different look on his face, and hands the phone to Mama, silently. She listens to her older sister, and starts to cry. Daddy and I are close as she sits down at the kitchen table, trembling, and crying. The crying is so sorrowful as she tells her sister....."At least we know where he is.....he's with Jesus. We'll be there in the morning." She hangs up the phone, trembling, and tells us, "Daddy died." Daddy and I feel helpless, unable to help in any way, except just to help her cry. I feel so sorry for her. I can't imagine her pain, and it frightens me something terrible when I think about me losing my Granddaddy, and any other member of my family. I just can't imagine, and I don't want to think about it---ever.

It's hard for me to fall asleep tonight. I keep thinking of all the good times I remember about Granddaddy. He was always smiling at us, especially the boys. He loved the girls, too, but I think he had a soft spot in his heart for boys, since all of his own children were girls. Mama and Daddy are still out in the playroom, so I can't really make out what they're saying. I guess that's a good thing, and a bad thing, at the same time. As I get sleepier, I think my best purpose of the day had changed a lot. Now I think my best purpose of the day was just to help Mama cry, and that sets pretty good with me somehow.

Ah, it's morning time. As I wake up this morning, I kinda sorta feel like there's a cloud over my house, maybe it's a real thunderstorm, but as I open the blinds and look out the window, I see a sunny day. The same is true as I look out the other window. So it must just be me. As I wake up and realize what has happened, how can I say, "Good morning" to anybody! It's NOT a good morning!

Mama and Daddy are talking in the kitchen, so I get up and head for the bathroom. I then join them in the kitchen, and as I walk down the long hall, I smell Mama's coffee percolator doing it's job. The smell is really strong. I get to the breakfast room and see Daddy first. He reaches out and hugs me, but says nothing. Then, he says, "I love you, Boy." I return with the same response. I then walk toward Mama, and she grabs me, and really holds me tight, and says nothing. I can tell it's hard for her to even be standing up, fixing breakfast for us. Shouldn't it be the other way around? No, I guess she needs to be doing something normal, because she's just "got to." But not me, I feel some really abnormal stuff coming on in the next few days.

While she's holding me close, I say to her, "I'm gonna miss that special smell of that after shave he used to use." She likes that, and with tears in her eyes, says, "Me too, and you know what......he loved you so much!" I start to cry because I know that was true. This just doesn't feel right. It don't feel right at all.

They decide to go to Kilmichael by themselves, and leave Maggie and me at home. They recon that's the easiest way. The funeral will be tomorrow, and they will go today and take care of all that funeral stuff, along with the other sisters there. They will come home tonight. Kilmichael is about an hour away. It's really small. Just a few hundred people live there. It's not like here. West Point is New York City compared to Kilmichael. But there is a bank there, and it's called The Bank of Kilmichael. He started that bank a long time ago, and he was the boss. Mama always brags on him because during The Great Depression, he somehow figured out a way to keep the bank open. She says that was really unusual. I don't know about stuff like that. Mama says back then, most of the banks around those parts did close. Mama and Daddy leave about 10 in the morning. So, it's just me, Fella, Willie Mae, and Maggie.

Dogs, I think, have something. I don't have a clue what to call it, but they know when something is wrong. I saw Fella really close to Mama as they walked out to the car. She loves him, and he loves her. She gives him special treats, like ham hocks and stew bones when she is cooking. Fella is staying really close to me as I go outside. It seems like I don't have to say a word. He just knows. I start telling Fella my confusion about all of this. He listens quietly. He's really a good listener. Maybe I ought to learn something from that. Daddy always says, "You're not learning when you're talking." I guess he's right. He usually is. Fella just seems to want to say, "Masta, I love you and I'm a hurtin just because you are a hurtin."

Maggie stays on the telephone with her friends. I guess she's dealing with this in her way-----different than me, but the same amount of sad.

Willie Mae has fixed us Dinner. It's weird with just Maggie and me at the table. I can't tell anybody how many times we have asked Willie Mae to sit with us at the table. But no. It's her choice to eat in the laundry room. That's just her way. The food is just as good as usual. Maggie says the blessing, and we eat. When we're finished, we take our plates to the kitchen, as usual, and we both tell Willie Mae, "Thank you." Then Maggie says, "You wanna go see a movie in Starkville or Columbus?" I say, "Sure, what you wanna see?" She says, "Love Story." I don't know nuthin about it, but it really don't make any difference to me. I just want to get out of the house. I say, "Sounds fine."

She looks at the daily newspaper, The Daily Times Leader, and then says to me, "It starts in Columbus at 3." That's perfect timing.

The ride to Columbus is pretty quiet. But I pay close attention to the area as we get close to the River, The Tombigbee River. It's higher now because of rains last week. I know there's a lot of activity underneath the surface of that water.

We get to the theater, go inside and get our tickets. The movie starts with a couple of cartoons, and then there is an announcement about what's going on in the Viet Nam area. There's been a lot of talk about that recently. But right now, we both are ready and willing to be "taken away" for a couple of hours-----just to get away from thinkin too much.

This girl in the movie. Her real name is Ali McGraw. She's real pretty. Some parts of the movie are really funny, and I like that. Now it's getting sad because she's getting bad sick. I DON"T need this, so I take a hike to the bathroom to get ride of that Coke I got earlier. I buy some popcorn while I'm out there. The smell is just too much for me to resist. It tastes really good.

By the time I get back, I see Maggie crying. I whisper, What's wrong?" She whispers back to me, "She said, 'Love means you never have to say you're sorry.'" I'm thinkin to my self, "What a pile of bologna! That's a bunch of hooie! Never having to say your sorry? That don't make much sense to me at all. When somebody wrongs me, I want to hear, 'I'm sorry.'" I liked the first part of the movie, but not the last.

We go to the shopping center in Columbus. Maggie is looking for some ear rings. The ones she's lookin at would work just fine as fish bait if they just had a hook in them. I leave her and head for the sports section. I am mainly interested in looking at the rods and reals. Getting a new reel sounds nice. I see some really nice ones. I see some made by Mitchell, some by Garcia, Zebco, and some others made by Johnson. I have a Johnson Century. It works just fine. It's not that I NEED a new reel, I just guess I WANT a new one, to make Paul jealous. I'm sounding like what Mama acts like when she goes into a shoe store. But there's a difference. She just lets that WANT overpower her. It's so funny to me. She has more pairs of shoes than Carter has pills.

When we get home, Mama and Daddy are already there. Everybody smiles, just glad to be together. That feels a little more normal. They tell us the service will be tomorrow at 2. We will leave early in the morning and will be with all the Kent side of the family.

Black people are a little different than us whites when somebody dies. Even if a black person dies on Monday, they wait till Sunday for the service and to bury them. And they grieve different than us, too. They just let it all out. And its a lot louder, too. They wail and moan. Our good friend, the Black undertaker, is Alvin Carter. He's a fine fella. He's really busy on Sunday though, I bet he has 5 or 6 services that day. That car he uses to carry the dead people? He uses that car as an ambulance service during the week. I don't recon if I broke my leg and needed to go to the hospital I'd want to ride in that car. It just don't seem right for some reason. There's been too many dead people in there.

Now it's the day of the funeral. I get up a littler earlier to feed Fella, 'cause we'll be gone all day. I rummage through the frigerator and find some good leftover stuff for him. Fella eats what we leave behind. It's funny to watch him eat collard greens. He seems to like them better than me.

The only thing I have ever seen that he won't eat is pickled beets. I can't say I blame him. Those things are just awful.

We leave the house about 9. We go by and pick up Willie Mae. She's in a fine Sunday dress. She's just like a member of our family, and she'll know a bunch of people there 'cause over the years they've been to our house. And Willie Mae loved Granddaddy, too. And he loved her. When they got to laughing together, it was really funny. So its Mama, Daddy, Maggie, me, and Willie Mae. Ruth, and her new husband David will meet us there.

On the way to Kilmichael, we pass under the Natchez Trace. I always like to see that. I would really like to go arrow-huntin along that pathway. I have a great collection of arrowheads. They are from many different tribes.

We arrive at Grand Mama's house. There are already a bunch of cars there. I can tell from the cars that the three sisters are already there. I know Gran Daddy has a special place in Heaven 'cause God gave him 4 girls, and no boys!

We walk up the squeaky wooden stairs to get to Grand Mama's front door. I know just which boards to walk on just to make them squeak. Those boards are really creaky. I'm sure Grand-mama and Grand Daddy knew when somebody was comin up those stairs 'cause they make such a racket. But mostly, everybody who knows them comes to the back door.

Right quick, we see Mama's 3 sisters and their husbands. Sister, Pretty Baby, and Eelii all give me big hugs. And their husbands shake my hand. Now I see all my cousins, too. Grand Mama comes to me, smiling really big. It's the kind of smile that says, "I don't care what you do, what you say, what you do in life, or what you don't, I will always love you all the time, always, no matter what!" She gives me the biggest hug, my insides hurt. She's a big woman, tall and big boned. She is bigger than Grand Daddy. He was normal size.

As I watch Willie Mae headed back to the kitchen to see her friends, I get a grin. I see Cloddy, Grand Mama's helper, and Honey Boy, her other helper. I love to see all them together. They seem to have more fun than anybody else. I've known Cloddy and Honey Boy all my life. They are very special to me. Once a week every Summer, I come here to visit. It's a blast. The adventures Grand Daddy and Uncle C would take me on are so fun. I hope those weekly visits won't stop now.

It's really hard to tell the difference from the cookin that comes from Cloddy's kitchen compared to the cookin that Willie Mae does. There's a difference, but they're the same. But whatever comes out of either kitchen is fine stuff. I just sit back in amazement watching them simply enjoying each other.

There's something very, very different about Honey Boy. Grand Mama really raised him 'cause his parents both died from "the fever." Daddy has told me Honey Boy is probably the most different kind of human he's ever known. Daddy has explained to me that Honey Boy is really, really lucky to be alive, 'cause he don't have what everybody else has. Daddy says when we sweat, it's our body cooling itself off. Daddy calls them "sweat glands." I don't know much about that. I just sweat. But Honey Boy don't sweat. He can't. His body don't have those glands to sweat. Daddy says most people like this die early 'cause they get too hot and they die. But not Honey Boy. Honey Boy is different. In the Winter, it's not problem. but in the Summertime, when he's workin in the garden, he can somehow tell when his body needs to cool off. There's a big watering pond for the barnyard animals right by the garden. Many, many times I have seen Honey Boy drop his shovel and run really fast and throws himself in that pond. After a few minutes, he's sunny-side up, just smilin really big with what few teeth he has. Daddy says that every time he does that, he's really saving his own life. And he does that 3 to 4 times a day! Grand Mama makes him eat outside 'cause he's so muddy. That don't seem to bother him a bit. He's probably the happiest person I know. Seems like he's just happy to be alive.

There's Dinner before the funeral. There's a bunch of food here. The Preacher is here, and he asks everybody to join hands and bow their heads.

He says the blessing......giving special thanks for life of Bertram Spivey Kent. Now it's really quiet. My cousin Murphy, Jr. breaks the silence and says, "Let's eat!" We sit down and dig in.

About 1:15, everybody there....all the family, all the helpers, start the walk down the hill just a little ways to the Methodist Church there. That's a very special place for our entire family, on both sides. All the helpers sit with the family.

This small church is really, really old. This is the same church Mama and Daddy grew up going to, and got married in. Same way for their parents, too.

This church is packed. All the seats are taken, and there are people standing on the outside of the pews. Maggie whispers to me, "There's a bunch more outside that just can't come in. I feel sorry for them, 'cause I know they loved Grand Daddy too, just in a different way."

The Preacher stands up, and speaks loudly. He tells those outside to come in and sit in the choir loft, to make room for everybody who can get in. He tells somebody to hold the doors open so if anybody can't get in, they can still be a part of it.

He begins the service by pointing to Granddaddy's casket and saying, "Don't think for a moment that Bertram Spivey Kent is layin in that box! That's only his shell! The real Bert's spirit has risen and is staring at the face of Jesus Christ right this very moment, and both of them are a 'smilin bigger than you can imagine!"

The Preacher says, "Let's sing Bert's favorite Hymn, 'Holy, Holy, Holy', page 64." He continues, "Let's celebrate his going home party!"

Everybody pops up like a jack-in-the-box. The organist pumps air in the pipes and out comes a tune I know very well. The Preacher is singin really loud, and he's raising his arms as if he's sayin, "Ya'll sing LOUD!" So everybody's singin really loud! I ain't never heard or seen anything like it before. I'm so glad I'm not sittin next to my Daddy right now. He can't carry a tune in a minnow bucket! I don't guess Jesus cares much about that, tho.

I thought this was going to be really sad, but this Preacher is turnin this thing into a party! I silently ask myself, "Am I TOO White 'cause I've only seen Black people do this. After the hymn, the Preacher starts to clap and says for all of us to do the same. Now everybody's standin,smiling, and clappin at the same time! It is so fun!

He tells us to sit down as he says, "Now you just got a little peek of what's goin on in Heaven right now!"

He says some comforting words to all of us in the family. He then says several funny things about his friend Bert. Like the time Bert was serving Communion and tripped, and grape juice went a flyin all over the first 3 rows.

Then he tells, "Bertrum ran the bank in town during the Great Depression. He fought really hard to keep it open when most of the banks 'round Misipi were closin fast! He

WON! Did you HEAR me, HE WON!" Everybody starts clappin again. He says, "If that bank had closed, Kilmichael would be a ghost town right now." Everybody is still clappin.

The Preacher continues, "Do you know another person who could have been a better father to those 4 girls and raised those 4 girls to be 4 fine women and still have a beautiful wife like Willie?" There was such a silence in that room that would scare some people. He said a few more comforting things, and closed the service with this:
"Bertrum did all these 3 things very well. Number 1. He lived justly. Number 2. He loved Mercy. Number 3. He loved The Lord God Almighty with all of his mind, his spirit, and his body."

Then he said, "Go in Peace, and do likewise."

The family got up first and walked out, then everybody else. Our family stood outside the church vistin with friends from long ago.

After the vistin at the Church, all of us got together and walked up the hill back to Grand Mama's house.

We all got in our cars and went to the Kilmichael Graveyard. By the time we got there, some folks had already brung Grand Daddy's casket.

The Preacher sits the family. There's so many people here, I can't count 'em all. The Preacher starts by grabbing a clump of dirt and says, "From clay we come, and to clay only our bodies return, but not the Soul. The Soul goes to God." He then rubs the dirt onto the closed casket and reads several verses from The Holy Bible. I can't 'member 'em all. I don't know most of them.

After he's finished, people start leaving. We know that Grand Mama is going to stay with "Sister" for a few days. She and Uncle C live just across the pasture at the end of the water pool.

After all the vistin, Daddy gathers the family and start to get our things and head for home. I got so many kisses from aunts, cousins, Uncles, I think I might just faint. And I know I am covered with lipstick and smell of perfume. My allergies are acting up so I can't tell if I smell like a tulip or not.

As we all get in the car, Daddy backs out of the driveway and heads down the hill we just walked up. He stops at the stop sign where the church is on the corner. He turns to Mama and says, "Beulah, we have had some life-changing things happen to us in that tiny church. May we cherish every one of them."

He takes a right, as usual, and heads for downtown Kilmichael. The main street of this tiny town of off the main highway. The main street is bumpy, with pot-holes. There is hardly any traffic right now.

As Daddy is driving and cruising through town, we see the bank....he stops....Mama tears up but it doesn't last long. While stopped, he asks Mama, "Do you mind of I drive by a few places while we are here?" She answers, "I wish you would, because the children haven't seen what I think you want to show them." He sez, "You're right, as usual."

Daddy turns the car around, and after a little ways, we see a row of really old red brick buildings. Some of the bricks are missing. Daddy explains, "My Daddy built all these red buildings, and he and some helpers built them from the ground up." "Look upstairs there," he says, and continues, "That's where my Uncle Reese had his drug store, and in the back of the drug store was my Daddy's medical office." He sez, "Now, look two doors to your left." I pointed left, thinking my sister Maggie didn't know right from left. Suddenly, I am bent over in pain from a punch in my ribs, and Willie Mae sez, "There they go agin, fightin like cats and dogs!" Mama and Daddy chuckle as Daddy sez, "Two doors down on the left was where my Uncle Ples had his dental office. His real name was Pleasant, but everybody called his Ples." He sez, "Uncle Ples has pulled a few of my teeth when I wuz your age." Mama chimes in, "And a few of mine, too." Mama and Daddy went to the same High School, but Daddy is four years older than Mama. Daddy was the quarter-back of the football team. So, it wuz the town's only Doctor's son marrying the banker's daughter. His family...4 boys. Her family...4 girls. What a story.

Daddy sez, "Now we're goin to see our old ranch, where our house use to be." We drive uphill on a narrow dirt road. Maggie sez, "Used to be, what happened?" Daddy sez, "It burned completely down, but only after Mama had sold it." Daddy continues, "After my Daddy died, my Mama moved into town 'cause she couldn't do all the ranch stuff."

It's a beautiful place to see. There are small rolling hills and on top of one of those hills, we see the ruins of what was their home. We get out of the car and walk up to the top of the hill. There are still big burnt timbers there. While Daddy is walking, he's telling us the way it wuz when he was growing up. He sez, "We had a one-acre garden," and points to a bare spot. It's a little bit away from where the house was. I see no trees around where they had the garden. Daddy told me they pulled them all up with a strong mule. I can't imagine how hard it was for them. The four boys tended the garden.

Daddy then takes us to the place where the barn used to be. Daddy has some really good memories from that 'ole barn. He sez, "My mama gave me a violin when I was small, and I guess I was really bad at it, 'cause the barn is the only place where they would let me practice." The barn had two levels, he sez. On the first floor, they stored all their tools, and stalls for the prized horses. Daddy sez, "The first floor also is the place Pop stored a special belt for when one of us boys acted up. He'd take us in one of those horse stalls and wear our behinds out!" Mama sez, "My older sister "Sister, can tell tales of your Daddy bringing a pillow to school with him after one of those spankins." But then Daddy jumps in quick, "But ya know something, after he's spank us hard, he'd then turn us around and hold us so close it scared us. Then, he'd say, 'Boy, I love you and nothing you ever do, think, or act, or say is ever going to change that." Then

Daddy gets a little choked up and sez, "I've never known a man like him. All the boys and Mama adored him." He continued, "Pop had the horse corral over there." He tells us, "It was a big circle with pole in the middle. Pop would work with those horses, training them."

But then Daddy sez, "But those horses in the pasture, when they saw Pop walk out of the corral, they stopped whatever they were doing and stood motionless, because their master was out of the corral. Pop could walk, with a bridle in his right hand, to any horse in that pasture, put a bridle on him, and hop on bare-back back and ride to the barn." "Even the horses knew who the boss was, and showed their obedience and respect without uttering a sound," Daddy sez. I agree. Daddy continues, "Pop would pick out a horse to just ride or to hook up to his buggy." Pop used that buggy to make house calls. Daddy sez, "That's just the kind of respect they showed him, not because of anything he said or did, but just for who he was."

Daddy then changed directions with his story-telling of the ranch. He said, "Back behind the house all the chickens ran loose. Mama would whistle and rattle a small sack of corn to draw them near. One time, I saw my Mama really, really surprised. I saw her catch a chicken by its wing, and then she grabbed that chicken by the neck, and walked, hatchet in hand, toward the chopping block." Laughing, he continues, "I saw this happen with my own two eyes. My Mama chopped off the head of this certain chicken, and then that chicken ran all around the barnyard with no head!" Daddy sez, "I have never seen a more surprised look on any woman's face like I saw that that. I think that look would have even scared Jesus." Then he sez, "Then, of course, the body fell, and she told me to go get it. I did." I wuz laughing so hard I know I did something in my pants."

Daddy points to a place a little further away and sez, "Our water well was right over there, and there was a natural spring right next to it....let's walk over there." Sure enough, we could see what used to be a well. Daddy walks a little faster, and says, "Come here. Here's the Natural Spring." He sez, "That's the purest water on Earth." The water just kinda bubbled up from below. It is bluish and crystal looking. We tasted it. It tasted different. Not better. Not worse. Just different.

He then says, "Come on, there are two more things I want to show you." I can tell Mama is getting a kick out of this. We all get back in the car, and drive up a pretty good sized hill on this dirt road. Maggie and I have no clue what he's up to.

At the top of the hill, he stops the car. He tells us to get out of the car and turn around. We finally see what he's about to explain to us. He says, "See that big hole? That's where the meteor hit!" Maggie and I look at each other and I ask, "What meteor?" Daddy sez, "Thousands, maybe millions of years ago a burning star fell out of the sky and what was left of it hit in that very spot!" Mama sez, "It musta been a mighty big one to make a hole as big as that."

Maggie and I take it all in. This is really interesting. We could really see the outline of some big object that God let fall out of the sky. Maybe it had done its job. Mama and Daddy smile at each other at the top of this hill. No need nor want to ask any questions 'bout that.

Daddy tells us to get in the car 'cause there's one more place he wants us to see. We drive up a hill on this bumpy road. We go maybe two miles, and then he stops the car, and tells us to get out.

We all do. He then goes to the right of the car. We follow him. We start to see gravestones. As we get closer, we see what looks like a sign with some kudzu growin on it. I tear off the vine, and it sez, "Flowers Cemetery." Maggie and I had no idea this was here.

Daddy sez, "Your ancestors are buried here." As we walk further into it, we see that all the tombstones had the last name "Flowers." There must have been hundreds of them.

We see, John Erasmus Flowers, 1825-1872. We see Sally Knox Flowers, 1790-1838. The list goes on and on. Lots of them make us think they were buried here after being killed in the Civil War. Some of the tombstones have Rebel signs on them. Others go even further back. We see some dated 1732-1757. Maggie tells me that's before the United States was a nation.

The smaller stones were closer together, and they were harder to read, but we could tell the dates. Some were 1870-1870. Others were 1882-1886. We quickly know these were the graves of children. And there are lots of them.

Daddy walks over and simply sez, "The Fever." He tells us that fever killed hundreds of thousands of people.

He walks over to a place like he's been there before. We are right behind him. We see the taller tombstone. It read, "John Harvey Flowers." We instantly know that was "Pop." Daddy stood there with us for a moment, and then knelt down, and put his head between his knees, and we can see his body shaking while he is crying. Mama quickly gets to him to comfort him. We see another stone beside Pop's. It's unmarked. Maggie tells me that's the stone waiting for Mam-maw, his mother. She is still alive. Willie Mae is bothered to see Daddy upset. She almost worships him.

With no sound, Daddy gets up, and heads for the car. We follow. Now we know we are headed for West Point.

This day is the most different one of my life. Interesting and scary. I think I did every emotion known to man today.

###Author's present day reflection: 1)Knowing when to go with the flow is a must, 2) Hurting people mourn unique only to themselves, 3)How easy it is to find blessings, 4) Celebrating the good exit from this life...somber, but not sad, 5) History, while valuable, is malleable as it blends with the present in anticipation of the future, 6) Respect.

Chapter 5
Age 12
"EUGENE THE MULE"

My uncle Harvey, my Daddy's younger brother and medical partner, has a small ranch/farm about one mile outside of town. To get to their place, we would have to get onto the familiar highway Miss. 50 East. There was a pretty good sized hill in the road, and at the top of that hill was the turn to their gravel road, to the left. That hill was called Hampton Hill. I know not why. I often wondered. Nobody around there was named Hampton.

Before one would enter their property, they would have to cross a wide "cattle gap."A cattle gap is actually a very short piece of road, built out of metal posts placed placed in a horizontal position. There were spaces between the round pieces of iron, wider than their hooves, which prevented a cow or horse from crossing that area looking for "greener pastures" and getting hit by a car. And that cattle gap was really bumpy. And the metal posts always looked rusted and old. But they served a purpose.

The gravel road to their house was only wide enough for one car, so if someone was leaving as we were coming in, one of us would have to move over into the grass and let the other car pass. And then the tires would get these thistles in the grooves of the tread, but did not pose any danger, they just looked weird. Just along the road a bit, the road splits, and the road to the left goes to the barn, where the horses are kept, and the road to the right goes to the house.

When it was Mama and me, I knew for sure we were going to the house. She would not have been caught dead intentionally going to a barn. That was not her style.

As we got closer to the house, the alarm bells went off! Not really alarm bells, that's just what I called their 2 German Sheppard guard dogs. And those two dogs came from the same litter as my dog Fella, but they were trained radically different. These were mean dogs, and everybody knew not to mess with them. They were not pets. They were on chains, tied to a big tree. And something really strange struck me. My uncle was a little unique, like my dad. He named his dogs' really dumb names. These dogs were named Fred and Zero. When I asked him why he named one Zero, just as a matter of fact, he told me, "He has no sense." I wish I could name some people "Zero." They were active dogs, so they wore the grass down to the dirt, so there was a distinct circle which was their domain. I would see green grass and then it stopped. They remained there night and day. And as we would drive by, they would bark loudly, with no harmony, and if there was a breeze, I could smell the stench they made just because of their existence. And it was bad. They were fed once a day, and were given plenty of water to withstand the summer heat. And there was a little hut set a little off the ground for them to climb into during the rain and cold. Boy, was it fun to see them during and after a nice rain. Their dirt turned to mud, and everything had black sticky mud on it, and the dogs would slip and slide around.

My aunt Ruth usually came outside to greet us and calm down the dogs, which she did quite well. Then we'd go inside through the side door. And in the winter, a fireplace was the first thing I walked by, and it was always going. Always. Like we did, they kept a fire going by putting a "back log" in the back of the fireplace. It was always a really big log, sometimes too big for me. And those logs were semi- seasoned, meaning that wood had been cut months before but there was still enough moisture in it to make it burn slowly. Then in front of that back log were the more "green" logs, those which recently had been cut and had most of the moisture still in them. Then on top of the green wood, was the seasoned wood. That combination meant there was always a warm fire to warm up some frozen fingers and toes.

And then my eyes would always wander upward to look at the brick mantle.

On top of that mantle laid a loaded shotgun. I knew why it was there, simply for protection, from varmints and other strange things. But it always has been interesting to me.

In the summertime, Aunt Ruth always had cold lemonade on-hand. It was made for the helpers who worked there, keeping the house and horses. I helped myself. And that lemonade was good, really sweet and iced cold and parts of the lemon remained in it.

After all the hello's and how-do-you-dos, I would go out the same door I entered, and headed straight for the barn. It was about a 75 yard walk, and on my right I passed a huge patch of bright green bamboo, stretching at least 15 feet tall. Occasionally, I would detour into the patch just for the short term entertainment of the density of the shoots, and the coolness caused from the blocking out of the sun. For a moment, I felt like Tarzan of the jungle about to do battle with a lion. But that was not my mission; my mission was to get to the barn. As I approached the barn, I see and hear activity. There are horse trainers and horses, and helpers.

This was a horse barn, and it had about 8 stalls. On average, they had about 5 horses in the barn, and 5 roaming around in the green pasture nearby. All of them were show horses, not normal riding horses. But they were still fun to rub, and they loved it as much as I did. Their skin was usually auburn in color, and felt like smoothed velvet. And their manes and tails were combed to perfection. These were Tennessee Walking Horses. These horses were specially trained to, upon a certain command, walk in a most unusual way. Their front feet rose as high as they could with every step. It looked almost like a strut. A really big strut. And these horses were being trained to hopefully win a prize in a horse show. This was my uncle's hobby. I would occasionally go to a horse show knowing he was riding that night. He was all decked out in a long black suit, long shiny black boots, and wore a top hat. We didn't do much teasing about that, although I really wanted to.

It was also really entertaining when the horse Farrier would come to the barn. They had a special area just for that purpose, properly shoeing the horses. The Farrier was called in and he would get to work. And it was dirty work, and the fire he used to melt and mold the steel shoe was the hottest fire I had ever seen. He even had to wear special clothing, protecting him from the heat, including a special mask to guard his eyes. I looked from a distance.

Earlier I mentioned the other 5 horses roaming around in the nearby pasture. There's where the entertainment really began for me. In that pasture were the 5 horses "in waiting". And there was also Eugene, the resident mule. Eugene was distinctly different. He is not a horse nor a donkey. But he was the product of the union of a horse and donkey. Both a horse and a donkey are pure blooded. Eugene was not. Mules are born sterile, so they cannot reproduce themselves. And they are built differently as well. Mules are bigger and stronger than a horse, and can physically do more work than either a horse or a donkey. But they are not known for their smarts. In that department, they are one taco short of a combo plate.

But, Eugene was fun. He was fun to ride. He was fun to walk, and occasionally I would get him into a short run, although he really didn't like to run and did not hesitate to let me know that. Can we say "stubborn?" We teased Eugene without mercy, and he did not react negatively at all. He just enjoyed having me and other people around, petting him and paying attention to him. When I looked at him head on, I would burst out laughing, because the first thing which comes to mind is, "This mule really looks stupid". He has a broad, ugly brown face, and his eyes were set wide apart, and a little bit cross-eyed. And his head is huge, way out of proportion to the rest of his body.

My uncle had Eugene there for a special purpose. No, he could not be trained to do much of anything. But sometimes a tractor overturns and ends up in a ditch. That is a really difficult situation. No human has a chance to pull it out, and no truck could get to it. That's when Eugene willingly came and did what he did best, using his God given talent for good.

He would be led to the mishap, then a bit and bridle would be put on him. And then a blanket and then a western style saddle. A western style saddle is different from most others. It has a "horn" at the front of the saddle, allowing a rope to be tied on it and then tied onto the object to be pulled. In this instance, a tractor was the object to be pulled out of the ditch. Eugene probably didn't know what or why he was pulling backwards with a tight rope. He just did it. And he also didn't know or care about all the cheers when his super human efforts succeeded with little effort of his own. Also, he didn't know or care when people like me teased him unmercifully.

The horses were beautiful, and in a way, so was Eugene.

He was my favorite. But we still teased him.

###Author's present day comment: 1) In a particular situation, another person would be a better fit for that unique job, 2) Sometimes, it's better to back off and let it happen. We don't always have to be in charge.3) Acceptance.

Chapter 6
"The Influence of Dr. Chester Swor"
Age 13

In Jr. High school, my body starts to change. Daddy warned me of this. I have a little fuzz on my face, pimples that I cover up with my sister's make-up, and glasses. I was not cool to myself, so I thought I probably was not cool to anybody else either. Last night I got a big surprise. I confused even my own Dad. I asked him, "Why do people have hair around their private parts?" He looked at me, a little dazed, and said, "I simply don't know."

I am confused about most things. I am certain of just a few things. My emotions are up and down, then down and up. But I let no one see any of this. Being seen sometimes is worse than not being seen. It works against me both ways.

West Point Junior High is located near the center of town on Westbrook Street. The Jr. High was bigger than the elementary school I attended. In elementary school, I knew everybody, and everybody knew me. That was not the case in Jr. High. Jr. High had students from the two elementary schools in town, and suddenly I did not know everybody. My world is larger, scarier, and full of change. Now I am changing classes every 50 minutes. I heard that changing classes was fun, and to some degree it was, but it was a chore to get to a class on the opposite end of the school in 3 minutes. But I had to visit with just a <u>few</u> people!

The school has two fire escapes. They are located on the second floor, on opposite ends of the school. The floors of the school are made of hardwood and are really cleaned each Tuesday after school. The smell of the stuff they used must have had some pine in it, because for a couple of days, I smelled pine. And I had a locker where I put my stuff. My combination lock is 487. After school, I sometimes find the classrooms where the escapes are...unattended. That is "the" moment of opportunity. We open the window to the escape, and climb into the metal cylinder, and enjoyed a nice ride down to earth. Then on Saturdays, we sometimes ride by the school on the way somewhere on our bikes, and take a stop at the school and climb up the fire escapes and again enjoy the ride down, but not as much fun as climbing out the window. The school grounds had little to no grass. Too many feet trying to get to class on time make the grass no chance to survive.

The only air conditioned place in school is the principal's office, Mr. Punders. And, ironically, that's the last place I wanted to be. Mr. Punders was a really nice fellow, and I get along with him good. He was well liked by those who followed the rules, and hated by those who did not. In his office, there is a belt hanging on the wall in full view. It's a scary looking belt, long and wide leather, with a silver buckle. That belt had met the backside of young men who really played outside the bounds. I think most of us have a healthy fear of Mr. Punders.

My current science teacher is Mr. Pitt. He is new to the school and fresh from college. He teaches science in a way that makes it fun while hardly ever using that big green science book that mostly stays in my locker. He tells us about Irion's Belt with a story about a giant battle in the sky. The victor is Orion, and the belt is a prize after defeating a king in a different galaxy. And the way he explains underground lakes is fascinating. He explains how they come from exploding volcanoes and spreading new earth right on top of existing lakes and rivers. He explains that in most places, it's not hard to find fresh water just maybe 100 to 150 feet below. He also made a point to say Science and Religion were actually partners, not mortal enemies. He gives several ways to tell us how The Old Testament described the night sky, and how scientific facts did not bump heads with what the Bible says.

We have many class discussions about that, and that is what makes it so interesting, because he seems to enjoy our thoughts and opinions. He never scoffs at anything we bring up, as long as it is a reasonable thought.

There is a choir in the school, but I am in the mood to try something new. I try my hand at playing trumpet. Bad mistake. My lips stay sore and puffy. I use a tube of Chap Stick a week. My lips just cannot position themselves to get a pleasing sound from that instrument. The best player is

Scotty Allen. His Dad runs the white funeral parlor in town. He sits in the first place seat. There are 5 of us. I sat in the 5th seat. Not a good sign. Over the semester, I conclude that the trumpet and I simply cannot continue. So I quit. And I didn't even get to march.

Miss Bramsom is our English and Typing teacher this year. She is pretty and single. It seems so odd to me that it would be valuable to me later in life that I learn to type. I have not plans to be a secretary, so why would I want to type? It just doesn't make any sense to me at all. And if I have no aspiring notion to be another Shakespeare, a 300 word essay would be so not necessary. When told by Miss Bramson to write an essay, I tell Dave Riley, my good friend, my plan. It goes like this: "I have a motorboat. When the motor is on, it sounds like putt, putt, putt, putt, (and continue the putts, and I have my 300 word essay)."

Dave is not very encouraging of my brilliance this time. He even suggests that I keep my plan to myself. I am insulted. But English turns out to be not so bad. Miss Bramson is understanding and kind, and that makes a big difference.

On Thursday, I see something on the bulletin boards all around school. It is a pamphlet of a mandatory school attendance to hear a guest speaker next Monday. The speaker's name is Dr. Chester Swor. I have never heard of him, but did that make any difference? Absolutely not. I have no choice but to attend. The only good thing I thought at the time was that I would get out of Math and PE, and that wasn't all bad.

So, the weekend before wasn't anything to brag about. Then Monday comes. I have not forgotten the meeting, but Mr. Punders gets on the PA system early that day and reminds everybody. Mr. Punders has several announcements, mostly bragging on the football team even though they got pounded last Friday night by the Pontotoc Panthers. Also, he gives an opportunity to be a flag person. I immediately sign up for that. I thought it would be cool to raise the flag in the morning and then bring it down after school. I was right. It really was fun. I had no idea there was a special way to fold the flag, and I didn't know why the stars were there and the stripes somewhere else. I had to learn all that in Cub Scouts, but it was worth it. The only time if wasn't fun was the time I raised it half mast was after President Kennedy died. We all cried.

Later that day, about 1:30, we are called on the PA to assemble in the big auditorium. I put my books away and start that direction along with everybody else. The seats in the auditorium are bent wood bottoms and bent wood tops. The wooden bottoms fold up when walking room was necessary. They are not comfortable seats. I have a boney butt. Somebody with more padding on their bottom would not have the problems I do. Fortunately for me, there are not many long meetings in there. As I find my seat, I see two men on the stage, Mr. Punders and the guest speaker.

When we were all seated, Mr. Punders takes the podium and grabs the mike so he can speak into it. He gives everybody a welcome and then gave a nice introduction to our guest speaker, Dr. Chester Swor.

As this guest speaker slowly approaches the podium, I cannot not help but notice he is very crippled. It looks like it is painful for him to walk. His right leg is gnarled, and he uses a cane. He gets to the podium, and he looks like a white haired ghost. He first explains how he became crippled. He speaks softly of a disease that I knew had been conquered, but not by him, and his generation. Polio. He grew up in The Great Depression, and knew the terrible times. And then, when he gets into his message, he has more enthusiasm than I, and speaks uplifting, encouraging words to all of us. His frailties disappear. He is strong. He is mighty. He gives great hope and promise of the future, and most of all, he says to follow those dreams. Follow those dreams, for they did not enter your brain by accident. He says those dreams were planted in my brain for a purpose, a divine purpose, just for me and my destiny. And that no one else could fulfill my dream but me.

Then he gets into the heart of his message. He speaks about the power of the spoken word, and the power of the tongue. He speaks of the tongue being the rudder of a big ship. He especially speaks about the power of what we know as "cussing". He calls it by its rightful name: cursing. He says when we use curse words, we are actually putting a curse on someone or something. That is powerful! I didn't want anybody to be cursed simply because I was really angry at them. He first wanted to us to understand the power we had. WOW! I really had power? That kind of power? That really hit me.

And then he gives an alternative to young people cursing. He suggests that we do a little research and find an extremely intelligent way to convey the same message.

He continues to speak: For example, if you disagree with a person, in an unhealthy way you would call him an ignorant idiot. He suggested we try saying this: "lei è una persona ignorante". That made perfect sense to me. The person on the other side of my argument would really have to go to the dictionary to find out what I had just called him. And how cool was that? I really did have more control than I thought. But I still slip up sometimes, but I am careful not to slip up around my family. That would result in a quick, certain death.

This message has impacted me like none other, in a very different way. From now on, I intend to express myself in a way like he described. He has a real passion for people, a real passion for life, for the creator of life, and for people to really dig deep within themselves to find purpose, designed only for them.

Only later did I discover who he really was. He was famous. He travels around the nation speaking hope to young people. Well, he gave hope to me that day. And he still does.

###Author's present day reflection: 1) Emotions are not to be trusted, 2)Listen to the whole messages before passing judgment, 3) using profanity is a distinct sign of ignorance.4)Judging a person before I know all the facts is a big mistake.

Chapter 7
"Introduction to Playboy magazine"
Age 13

My 8th grade fall semester has just begun. It's still hot outside, but it's beginning to cool down at night. Labor Day has just passed. Pretty much all the businesses closed down for Labor Day. My Dad's clinic was closed as well, but a few random calls landed at my home.

During the early fall, we have some violent storms come through. We are at the bottom of the Jet Stream, which means we don't get a lot of violent weather, but when we do, it's intense. Last night was one of those nights. First it was the rain, and it really rained hard. And then I heard Mama voice concern about the upcoming winds on our tall pine trees. We have over 100 full grown pines in our yard. My dad planted them before I was born. They are huge, and give off a sweet smell, and their brown needles fall and make great ground cover, and are soft to walk on. These trees are absolutely gorgeous, but they are not made to withstand really strong winds. My Mama voiced a legitimate concern. After about 20 minutes of hard rain, then the winds came, as predicted, from the North West. The electricity was knocked out, so we had to go to the bottom drawer in the kitchen cabinet next to the stove to get the candles and transistor radios. We had two of them, gifts to my dad from one of the drug companies at Christmas. He always gets more Christmas gifts than anyone in the family. One of the radios had a fresh 9 volt battery, so we tuned into the local radio station, WROB, and listened to the announcer "Jack somebody," reading a weather alert from the National Weather Station, that was in Memphis, 150 miles North of us. The local station could only give us what was fed to them, 'cause they have no equipment themselves. So, we listened carefully as the winds grow more and more strong. Then we started to hear very clearly what we did not want to hear...cracking limbs, falling limbs. My mother loves those trees, as all of us do. The winds continue for about 45 minutes, and then subsided some and the storm moved eastward toward Alabama. It's about 10 o'clock at night and it is still really gusty, and the rain had stopped. Mama asked me to go outside and check on the trees. I went into the utility room, reached up into the white cabinet where she stored the laundry soap, grabbed the big flashlight, and put on a light jacket and went out onto the back patio. That patio was in the back of out house, and I saw small pine tree limbs on the patio. But that was not my concern. The bigger ones were toward the back edge of our property, and that was where I was headed. As I walked, I knew the drill. I knew pine trees either break or they don't. And that's the story. I was looking not whether or not we lost some limbs, but how many. As I continue, I feel a sigh of some relief. I find one broken one on the west side, one on the back side, and one on the east side, but no trees down. On a relative scale, I considered this a victory. I then go back into the house to report to my Mama. I told her we only lost 3 limbs. She tried hard to see the blessing of that. But the storm was over, and we go to sleep with the electricity off. But it came back on before we got awake. The big clock above the TV was off its time. I reset it. That clock is shaped like a star, very black, and its hands were gold colored. It's been there longer than me.

Today is Wednesday. We got registered for all our classes last week. That went well. I got positioned in classes among as many pretty girls as possible. The mission was accomplished. That was especially true in English, where I was to sit by Shelley, who was far and away the cutest. She paid some attention to me, but not quite enough.

My bike and I are still best pals, along with Fella, my faithful dog. I will not get my driver's permit until next year. I can't wait. But for now, my bike will do just fine. As I begin my ride to school from home, I notice the streets are still wet from last night's storm, and as I travel on the sidewalk, I have to dodge some downed limbs. I turn around briefly to see Fella in the background, following me. He sometimes follows me all the way, sometimes not. Today he did not. He went back to the house to wait for me to return later in the afternoon. It takes me about 10-12 minutes to get to school, weaving through neighborhoods and side streets. I sometimes take a different route just to break it up.

Today, I did want to go a different route to see how many big branches were down.

As I pass McCord Street, I can hear the power crews out cutting limbs which were hanging, and as I cross Mc-Cord St., I see them. It's a crew of 3. I slow just a little to see the commotion, and then back on track. As I get closer to school, I am joined by 2 friends, Doug Riley and Dirk Germany, who were coming to school, but from another direction. We visit as we ride slowly, talking about the storm, talking about girls, and then Doug asked if we were really going to have an English test, or not? I was stunned, I had forgotten all about that blasted test. He mentioned she should not give it to us today because none of us had light to study. And I doubted very seriously that she would compare us studying like Abe Lincoln did, by candlelight. We all laughed, but hoped it was true. But, not worries for me, because I had Study Hall right before English, so I could get a little prepared.

Mr. Punders did his normal announcements on the PA system, and then we got down to the task at hand. This project in Science is building a model to show the distance and size differences between the Earth and Mars. It was a fun project.

The next class was Study Hall, so I quickly went over the test material Miss Bramson mentioned last Friday before Labor Day. It didn't seem too difficult, until I got to the section where I was supposed to know how to use the words "lay" and "laid." I was not so sure about that and have serious doubts that I ever will be.

That time went quickly, and the bell rang. I gathered my stuff, and headed for English class. Miss Bramson, our teacher, was young and single. She liked to joke with us. Today was one of those days. She actually had a burning lantern on her desk when we walked in. I smelled the soot coming from it. She was not smiling. As we got seated, she then smiled and said she did not expect us to be like Abe. We were relieved, and she gave us an open book test! WOW! She really gained some brownie points with me when she did that. I think I smoked it, all but the "lay", and "laid". I really had a problem with that.

Wednesday is one of the days I choose to bring my lunch rather than buy my lunch at the school. The lunch on Wednesdays is meat loaf, green beans, and carrots, and a roll. I know what good meat loaf is, and this stuff should not even be called meat loaf. It should be called "mystery meat." It is terrible. And, the green beans? I vowed never to eat their green beans after hearing from my older sister, Maggie, when she found a band aid in her green beans. That's a sight I do not want to see. I am content with my bologna sandwich, potato chips, and a piece of caramel cake. Mama had gone to the bakery at Mississippi State University and picked up a cake last Saturday. That was my favorite part of lunch.

The rest of the school afternoon was uneventful. After the 3:30 bell rang, I walked outside with my friends. It had cleared off from being cloudy earlier and now was sunny. And there was a slight wind. That was good news. Because I now knew I had a chance to go to the house and fly my kite. I love to fly kites. And I am really good at it. I take my normal route home, and things looked a little different than in the morning. Things had been cleaned up, and it was a nice day.

As I get closer to the house, I called out for my dog, Fella. That was normal protocol. And he ran quickly to join me, and we went on toward the seashell driveway. It had become sunny and I had to squint my eyes as I pulled up in the driveway. I put my bike away, and got my stuff and headed for the side door. Mama's car was in the driveway, and the door is unlocked, as it always is, and I walked in. Mama was in the kitchen doing something uninteresting, so we said hellos and I turned from the kitchen into the den, where the family spends most of its time together. First, there is Daddy's big chair on my left, and then a long coffee table full of magazines, face up, on top of it to my right. As I passed the table, I felt the blood flow completely out of my body as I saw right on top a PLAYBOY magazine! And it happened to me <u>mine</u>! I was stunned, I was shocked, I was SO busted! I shivered for a moment, gained my composure, and had to make a decision. My mom obviously put it there after finding it underneath my bed while cleaning my room. So, what do I do? Do I take it in the kitchen and talk with her about it? Do I remove it and go to my room?

I am so busted; I do not know what to do.

I decide to remove it, go to my room, and hide it AGAIN. But why should I hide it? They would just find it again. Was this MY room or not? Do I deserve any privacy? I'm thinking about a padlock.

In my room, it took me a few moments to think about this. I knew I had some explaining to do, but, but, this is big.

I went into the kitchen where my mother was, and she started small talk. She knew how uncomfortable I was. I responded with talk about school and the downed branches I saw on the way. Not a word was said about that magazine at that time. Not a word.

During the small talk, I mentioned I wanted to fly my kite. She mentioned I should go ahead and do that, so I bolted. I flew it for a while, but all I could think about was either Willie Mae or Mama cleaning in my room, and finding that magazine under my bed. And what would my sisters say about this, and what would my Daddy say? I was in sheer misery.

When my sister arrived, she pointed at me and laughed. I knew she knew. Now I was wondering who else knew? I suddenly became unsure of everything.

My Daddy came a while later. He drove up in his white Ford Mustang. He got out, waved hello and walked toward me. He leaned on Mama's car. He asked how about my day. He then said something which seared its way into the deep part of my brains. He told me that I was not evil for looking at that magazine. He told me the feelings I had were very normal. He totally understood what I was feeling. He then said men are more visual beings. He then said something really important. He said those feelings were normal for me, but it's what I DO with those feelings that's important.

And as for the padlock? He made it perfectly clear that the house was HERS, so don't even think about it. I got the message. And that was it.

When we walked inside, everybody was laughing. I knew they were laughing AT me, and not with me, but that was OK. Everything was out in the open. And it was cool. At Supper, I had to explain how I came up on that magazine in the first place. And everybody was smiling, including me.

The next day I decided that magazine had no place in my home, and I got rid of it.

####Author's present day comment: 1) Hiding info is not a good idea. The weight of the consequences are too great, 2) My limitations may not be as obvious to me as they are to others, 3) Listening to wisdom is important, 4) Instant forgiveness is wonderful.

Chapter 8
The Agony and the Extasy, 1967, Fall, age 13

Hunting will be big this fall because we have had really good rains this past Summer. Paul and I are in the playroom cleaning our guns, getting ready for the season. Daddy walks in, nods his head and says, "Sometimes emtpy guns kill people just as dead." That's his way of warning us to treat an empty gun as if it was loaded. I tell him, "We got the message, thank you." He sits down to watch the news as we continue to clean our guns. Daddy perks up to hear a story coming from South Africa. It's about a Dr. there named Dr. Christian Bernard doing the first ever heart transplant. He loves stuff like that. Also in the news, they are talking about Super Bowl 2. That's interesting, too.

Now the phone is ringing. Daddy gets up to answer it. It's his friend Thompson McClellan, a close friend and a local lawyer. Mr. McClellan is a little bit older than my Daddy, and went to Ole Miss, just as Daddy did. But I know what he's doing. He's inviting Daddy on a quail hunt. He loves to hunt quail with highly trained dogs. And I also know Mr. McClellan knows my Daddy does not like to walk for long distances. So, Mr. McClellan sometimes hunts quail on horseback, and that's when he calls Daddy to go with him. Fortunately, Daddy has the good sense to accept the invitation. Paul and I are very pleased. Daddy comes back in about to speak. I say, "We already know. When are you going with him?" Daddy laughs, and says, "Two weeks Saturday." Daddy is highly experienced on a horse because of his upbringing. He's hunted with Mr. McClellan like this before and comes home with quail, a sore shoulder and a sore behind. Daddy used to be a better shot than he is now, simply because of lack of going often enough.

Mr. McClellan only offers these types of hunts to special friends, and Daddy is honored to be invited.

Mr. McClellan's office is on Court Street, right across from the Court House. I remember that because I was his paperboy when I had my paper route a while back. I worked for the daily newspaper, The Daily Times Leader, and the Editor, Mr. Harris, was and is a good friend of my Dad's. I had the downtown route, the easy route. Every other paperboy rode a bike to deliver papers. But not me. I had a brown canvas bag, and it hung over my shoulder. I did that 5 days a week. I hated Thursdays because the merchants had all their specials for the week inserted, which made my bag much heavier, but it was still fun. I started at 11 am, and was done by 3, covering all of downtown. And it was good money, too. I earned about $35 a week. That was great spending money. All the merchants knew me, simply because of my Daddy. Most of them got in the habit of calling me "Little Doc." There's more evidence there was no value in my parents giving me a name. Nobody ever uses it.

I used to ride my bike to the paper office, then walk in and get my stack of papers waiting for me. Most of the time, the paper would run on schedule. Occasionally, they would run a little behind, and I would wait in the front office. The editor of the paper, Mr. Harris, would come out of his office and is it with me for a few moments. He and my dad are pretty close friends. I am highly suspicious that I got the job because of their friendship.

Across the street from the paper office is what everybody calls "Lawyer's Row." Most of the lawyers in town have their offices there, and they all seem to look alike. I guess they office there because it's right across the street from the county Courthouse and the street is named Court street. I wonder why.

In the courtyard of the Courthouse, there are two drinking fountains. The big one is for the bigger people, and the shorter one is one made for littler people. They have silver handles to turn on the water. Those white drinking fountains seem like they are made out of the same stuff that bathtubs at home are made of. Last year, that big sign around the drinking fountain which said, "For Whites Only" was removed. I am really glad. They seemed to take their sweet time removing it. Those fountains, on hot, steamy summer days, were a big help to me. Now they can be a help to everybody.

I started my paper route at the Courthouse, and delivered papers to all of the offices on all three floors. I don't have any clue what those offices are for. Some say, "Tax", some say, "License." I greet everyone and everybody greets me. I walk by the big court room every day. Sometimes a trial is going on, and that means there's a pretty big crowd of people walking around, and the courtroom is full of people. The court room looks like the one they used in the reruns of one of my Daddy's favorite TV shows, "Perry Mason." I never understood that show. Nobody could be right THAT often. Everybody's gotta lose some of the time. I don't get it.

The route was the same every week day. Lot's of times, when I would open a merchant's door, they would say, "Little Doc, your're right on time." Nearly every day I'd go into Harris and Riley Drug

Store, deliver their paper, then head for their Coke machine. There's was the coldest one in town, I think. I usually got a Coke or a Sprite. Then I'd either get a Butterfinger or some crackers with peanut butter in the middle. The favorite part was picking the Butterfinger pieces out of my teeth. After my route, I would usually go watch TV or fly my kite. My dog likes to go with me when I fly my kite.

This Friday night is quiet. We go out to eat Supper Mize's Restaurant, the local restaurant. The waitress seats us, and asks us what we want for an appetizer. Mama just tells her to bring me whatever they are having. I don't know what an appetizer is. The waitress returns with a salad with a creamy 'sumthin on top. I give a puzzled look at Mama. She says it's, "1000 Island Dressing, but it's just really Catsup and Mayonnaise mixed up." That's OK with me. We just don't eat salads like this at home.

Jimmy Mize, the owner, comes over to greet us. He and Daddy are friends. He has 5 children. After he leaves, Daddy says he delivered all 5 children. Mama says they are Catholic. What is the connection? I don't get it. But who cares? I'm hungry.

Daddy and I order the fried shrimp. Mama gets a small steak. After Supper, I am really full. When we get home, things are quiet until about 9:30. Daddy gets a call from the Emergency Room and hears what's going on. He hangs up the phone and say's, "C'mon, Boy."

Quickily, we go to the ER and find a fellow who was on the wrong end of a bad knife fight. He had 3 different cuts, but he was not in danger of dying. It didn't take Daddy long to sew him up with me cutting the stitches. We finish up and head for home about 11 pm. I am really tired and tell everybody G'night. Daddy is probably going to stay up and fix a sandwich, as if the shrimp wasn't enough.

It's Saturday morning, and I ride with Mama to go get Willie Mae. We get back around 9:15. About 9:30, Daddy gets a call from the ER at the Hospital. He is very quick to hang up and sez, "Come on, Boy, quick!" I run and put on my tennis shoes and jump in the car.

He drives faster than normal, so I know something really weird is going on. When we get to the ER, we go into the Exam Room and find his good friend Thompson McClellan on the table with his left hand covered up with bloody bandages. He sez to Daddy, "Doc, I shot off my fingers while I wuz huntin this morning." Daddy says nuthin and asks no questions, he just gets to work. He gently upwraps the bandage to find a bandage in a bandage.

One of the bandages contains what's left of 3 of his fingers, and Daddy opens the last bandage and finds a really messed up hand, with several fingers missing. He quietly examines it, and says, "Thompson, I need to send you to a hand specialist in Memphis." Daddy receives a quick, and direct answer, "R.B., you're my friend and my doctor. They ani't got nobody in Memphis that you can't do right here, right now, so just do the best you can!"

Dead Silence.

I know Daddy is a highly trained, highly gifted abdominal surgeon. He is not a hand surgeon. But here he is, hearing a close friend, say, "Do your best."

Daddy quickly changes roles. He tells the nurses to quickly get him to the operating room. He tells a nurse to call Mama to come and get me, because he's going to be a while.

While I wait on Mama, I think about what's going through my Daddy's mind right now. He is making a detailed plan on how best to help this man. His mission: reconstruct a hand and fingers the best possible way. Now that I think about it, Daddy did do a good bit of different kind of medical stuff while in Residency at Charity Hospital in New Orleans. He was Chief Resident there. But I'm not so sure he did anything like this, I don't think.

Mama arrives, and I fill her in as best I can. Now, she is worried for Daddy, but confident he will do his best, especially since Mr. McClennan did ask him to.

When we get home, my dog Fella greets me, and Mama and I go inside. It smells like Willie Mae is fixing some of her World Famous Pork Chops, and I also smell "hot water bread" (white corn meal with hot water and then fried to a crisp in the oven on a flat black iron skillet.)

On the opposite counter, I see chopped up pecans and the makings of Mama's World Famous pecan pies. I immediately ask Mama, "Who died?" She just smiles and says, "Nobody, it's just for us." This must be my lucky day. The reason I asked the question is that when someone we know dies, she always takes them a pecan pie, and we rarely get one, except at the Holidays.

At Dinner on this Saturday, Daddy's seat is empty and the phone doesn't ring. What an odd combination that is. Willie Mae's fried pork chops are wonderful. And the way she fixes those potatoes always sends me away full.

After Dinner, Willie Mae and Mama cut that special Pecan Pie. I ask Willie Mae, "Do we have any vanilla ice cream?" "'Sho do, Ray, and I'll get some, just for you." She knows me too well. That warm pecan pie and some vanilla ice cream sends me to the moon and back, It is soooooooo delicious. It's so rich I can have only one piece of pie, after those finger-lickin pork chops. I know if I eat too much ice cream, I'll get the runs. But sometimes it's worth it.

It's about 2 pm and Mama and Willie Mae have finished in the kitchen. And it's time to take Willie Mae to her house. I ride with Mama to get her home. I don't usually go with Mama, but at this late hour to get her home, I know her husband, Joe, who tends to the local jail, is out front in a tall rocking chair Daddy got for his bad back. When he sees us, he gets up, and slowly walks toward the car. He is so skinny, he would make a tooth-pick look fat. He is almost skin and bone, but he's healthy. When he gets to the car, he smiles and says, "Hi, Miss Beulah, and hello there, Grasshopper." He has called me that since I been able to remember. He says he calls me that 'cause when I was learning to walk, I hopped like a grasshopper. I don't remember that, but I do remember that he's just one more person who doesn't call me by my given name.

On this hot, humid Saturday afternoon, on the way home, I ask Mama to drive me by the "Big-R" drive in so I can get a grape snow cone. She says, " You gonna put grape snow cone on top of that pecan pie?" She's laughing while talking. I say to her, "It's all the same once inside." She chuckles and heads for the "Big-R." We drive up to the order-takin' window and a teen-ager on roller skates comes to us and says, "What can I get you?" Mama tells me to tell her what I want. I say, "I'd like a medium grape snow cone." Mama looks at me with those 'Mama alligator eatin' her young' eyes, and finishes my sentence sayin' "Please, mam." I say to Mama, "I forgot that time." She smiles and the roller-skatin' lady is back in no time with my cone. Not surprisin' or nuthin', Mama asks, "Can I have just one bite?" She does that every time.

As we drive into the driveway, we see Daddy's Mustang. We go inside.

I immediately start asking questions, and Daddy has a big grin on his face, and says, "Well, I was able to re-attach one finger and re-locate one finger, and I think he's going to be OK." I was stunned and said, "You re-located a finger?" He just says, "Yup." When I get a few more details, I am even more amazed. Mr. McClennan had shot off his little finger, and the one next to it, and 1/2 of the middle one.

What Daddy had to do was this; The little finger was history, beyond repair. He completely moved the middle finger and re-located the one next to it, and re-attached the nub left from that finger, so now he has a useful thumb, an index finger, and a new middle finger, although it turned out to be a little short. But who's countin'?

Daddy never brags on anything like that, but I could tell he was pleased with what he had done.

The next day, Sunday, a Church day, I see Mr. McClellan there with a big cast on his right hand and arm. And it was highly bandaged up. He comes over to me in the fellowship hall while I'm there getting a Sprite. He says, "Little Doc, yo Daddy really helped me yesterday. My shot gun went off while I was gittin' on my horse to hunt. I made a stupid mistake and shot my fingers off." He continues, "This cast will be with me for 6 weeks, your Daddys sez." I say, "Wow", and we go our seperate ways.

The six weeks go by quickly, and on a Saturday morning, Daddy asks me if I want to go with him to take off the cast. I respond, "I'm in the car!" We go to his office. Mr. McClellan was waiting for us. We all go into the exam room. Daddy then puts on his big plastic glasses to protect his eyes from the cast-cutter dust. Daddy then uses a really small saw, and cuts the entire cast off with one swipe. While he is taking off the bandage, he warns Mr. McClellan not to try to move anything quickly. He sez only small wiggles are necessary.

What I see now compared to what I saw 6 weeks ago is like night and day. This man had 3 fingers shot off, and now he has a right hand, not perfect, but very workable. Daddy had done a semi-miracle. The remaining fingers wiggle with no pain. Now this man has to train himself to write with the same hand he used to, but now it's a bit different.

From that moment on, he did not call my Daddy "R.B." His new nickname was "Hero." He's my Hero, too.

Part Two of.........."The Thrill of Victory and the
Agony of Defeat."

We all know by now that Mama makes the best pecan pie on the planet. I am quite confident that God Himself would yield to Mama in this arena. There's just no dispute. But when it comes to cakes, now that's a different story. No clue as to why or why not. On somebody's birthday, oh yes, there's a Birthday Cake, but not make with her precious hands, oh no. It would either come from the talents of Willie Mae following the directions on the box of Sara Lee. If it was a big birthday, she goes over to the bakery at Mississippi State University, just 18 miles away. She always buys a Caramel Cake, Chocolate Cake, or on rare occasions, a Coconut Cake. I have absolutely no objection to any of those she brings home. Nobody has recently died, so we have not seen any Pecan Pies recently.

At our local Methodist Church, every 3 months, there's a "family night" Supper. Everyone who comes brings a dish, and most of the time it's their "signature" dish. We had one of those last night, and I ate enough to fill 3 hogs. I had a "little bit of this," and a "lot of that," and seconds on many things.

One thing puzzles me. Last night, a member of our church, Lacey Wyatt, brought a Pecan Pie. I tasted it. It was identical to Mama's! My question would be; Who came up with that recipe first, Lacey or Mama? I don't feel the need to persue that can of sour worms.

Lacey's husband's name is Barley. Lots of people joked him that he really liked grains, because he worked in the School of Agriculture at MSU. The more I think about his name, it makes me think that if Barley had a younger brother, his name might be Soybean, or Corn.

Barley and Lacey are good friends of my family, on many fronts. Barley called Daddy a few days ago and expressed a health concern about their daughter, who was named after her mother, Lacey. Barley was describing Lacey having trouble with her vision. Daddy said to him to have her come to his office late in the day, the next day, so he could have a thorough examination of her.

Today is Monday. I am out of school for Christmas Holidays. I am sitting aroung the house today because I think I have caught a cold, or maybe it's just allergies. I do suffer from allergies in different seasons, but not to compare with the allergies Mama suffers from. My Mama constantly describes what she calls, "My snot rag," to wipe her nose when necessary. I have more dignity. I have a hankerchief in my right back pocket. With my cold/allergy, I have already gone through 3 hankerchiefs today. I think that may be a record.

It's kinda been a sad and unusual few hours. The morning was consumed by TV, and I have been reading an instruction booklet on how to play the game of Chess. A few of my friends have joined in, and playing Chess can occupy study hall, or a rainy day.

Dinner was good, I think. In fact, I am sure it was, simply because Willie Mae was involved. But the bad part is that I can't taste a thing. My nose is really clogged.

Daddy went back to the office a little earlier than normal after dinner because he knew Lacey would be waiting for him. Maggie had left with some of her friends, so it was just Mama and me after Mama had taken Willie Mae home.

About 3:30 in the afternoon, I hear a car in the driveway. He almost never comes home in the middle of the day. He opens the side door, doesn't utter a sound and immediately sits in his easy recliner. He puts his hands over his face, and starts crying intensely.

Both Mama and I immediately ask him, "What is it? What's wrong?' He says, "Gimmee a minute." He was trying so hard to maintain his composure, but just could not.

"It's Lacey, he said. He continued, "I think there is something seriously wrong with her, and I don't think I can help her." He continued, "What am I going to tell Barley and Lacey?" I don't want to tell them what I really think is happening, but I have to."

Mama asked him, "What do you think she has?" He hesitated to wipe some tears away and said, "I think she may have a disease that could eventually take her life." Mama started crying then and holds him close. I just can't rid of those cold chills up my spine as I hear this.

Evidently, Daddy had to come home for a few moments to "Let it out", and regain his composure. He loves this brillant young woman, full of life and hope for the future.

After a few moments of silence, he gets up and goes back to their bathroom and washes his face. He then goes back to the office to see those waiting for him to preform a miracle in their lives.

Seeing my Daddy like this, caring so much about was revealed in her exam was very revealing and reminds me of something which obviously has stuck through my thick skull. At church, I have heard Brother Dinas say something. He talks about the shortest verse in the Bible, which is, "Jesus wept."

###Author's present day reflections: 1)When I do a good job, it's OK to give a gentle pat on my back. Anything else inflates the ego 2)Find a really good candy bar and stick with it, 3) It's OK to cry and be sad when I discover that a situation is out of my control 4)When it's up to me to tell someone really bad news.

Chapter 9
"I look like a Haint"
Age: 13

My Mama's stirring about gets me awake me this summer morning. As I am stretching while still in my bed, my mom walks by my room, sees me awake and comes in to give me a "Good Morning" kiss. She still is in her robe. She says, "Hey there, big man" and then immediately follows that with "Forgive me, I know I look like a "haint." I laugh out loud and head for the bathroom. On the way, it hits me. I know now it's Wednesday. The reason I know is because that's the only day she says that. Thursdays at 2pm is the sacred time she spends with her dear friend Eloise at "Eloise's Beauty Shop". That's where she get her hair "done". I'm simply not capable of completely putting that puzzle together, but hey, I don't care to put it all together. It doesn't bother me, and God help the man or woman who try's to intrude on that 2pm Thursday appointment. I think that if I came in bleeding from a really bad bicycle wreck at 1:30 on Thursday, I know she would enlist my older sister or a total stranger off the street to take me to my dad's clinic for immediate medical treatment.

Back to the word "haint." That word is very familiar in my family's vocabulary and is totally understood when used either as a noun or a verb.

The origin of the word "haint" is haunt. I am keenly aware of the poetic license of the English language which only we Southerners can execute and enjoy, and successfully get away with it. We do it with great pride. When the word is used as a noun, it is to imply one is a "spook" or a "ghost". That's not a good thing. When the word is used as a verb, it is to imply one is doing something without purpose and is borderline irritating to someone nearby. My mother and sisters often complain of my dad "hainting" around the kitchen late at night. The kitchen at my house is a highly restricted area, such as the security around Ft. Knox, protecting the U. S. supply of gold. My mother abhors my Daddy in her kitchen. He is only allowed in the kitchen in her presence one day a year when he is allowed to fix his world famous seafood gumbo to celebrate Fat Tuesday during Madi Gras.

Now that I know it's Wednesday, I am a little more quiet than normal because I know my Daddy, an abdominal surgeon, is still asleep. Wednesdays are one of his days to operate on people. On Wednesdays, I know he is scheduled to operate at 11am. He purposefully schedules surgery later in the day because he's just not an early morning person. He's a night owl. I have two older sisters and they get really irritated when they come home from a date and bring the date inside only to find my dad "hainting" around the kitchen, building himself a hero sandwich. They continually gripe about that.

As I move toward the den, I turn to the right to turn on the TV. I flip around the 5 channels we have and stop when I find the 3 Stooges. I love to laugh, and they make me laugh really hard. I am waiting for my Daddy to wake up. I am waiting to have my breakfast with him. He spends so much time helping sick people, I take every opportunity I can to spend some time with my hero.

About 8:45, I hear him walking down the hall towards me in the den. He has to pass this way on his way to the kitchen. When he sees me on the floor watching TV, he leans over and scrubs my head and says "Hey boy." That's what he calls me, "Boy." I can't possibly remember the last time he's called me by my given name. Come to think of it, nobody in my entire family calls me by my given name. Why did they bother to give me a name?

When the feeling comes back in my head, I get up and join him in the kitchen. The smells are really fine coming from there. Mama has fixed home made biscuits and in addition, grits. Daddy and I fill our plates and take a seat. Daddy says the blessing, and Mama joins us at the breakfast table with only a cup of coffee. She makes the coffee each morning, and she makes it HER way, in a percolator. The strong aroma permeates through the house, and she's the only one who has the nerve to drink it because it's so strong. It's almost like a syrup. Daddy jokes her and says her coffee is the stuff Jesus Christ is going to use to wake the dead.

During breakfast, mama asks daddy what kind of surgery he's doing today. He tells her it's a hernia problem high in this person's abdomen. As we finish putting butter and pepper on our grits, he asks me, "Boy, what do you have going on today?" I respond with, "nuthin special." He then says "you want to scrub up and join and maybe help me in surgery? I jump on that opportunity quicker than I can pull my hand out of fire.

After we got showered and clean, we headed for the hospital at 10:28. We arrived at the hospital at 10:30.

He takes me into the prep room. He changes clothes into a smelly green suit and tells me to do the same. This green suit comes with a top with short sleeves and bottoms with a draw string to tighten up around my waist. I look really ridiculous because this suit was made for somebody much bigger than me. And if that's not enough, I have on red, white, and blue tennis shoes. I look like a flag from a foreign country. Anybody here with a camera will be shot dead immediately. We then walk into the scrubbing area. There's a white-faced black-handed clock on the wall. It reads 10:45. My dad sez, "We scrub for 15 minutes." I start at my elbows and suddenly realize my earlier shower at home was an act of futility. I felt sorry for the tiny hairs on my arms. And then came the hands and fingernails. There is a special brush just for the fingernails. I was thinking even the fish bait from yesterday was about to be washed down the drain. I am quite sure my fingernails have never nor ever will be this clean again. At 11:00, we stop and Daddy says "Put your hands up like you're being arrested," and then laughs. A nurse with a mask on her face opens the operating room door with her foot, and as we pass I can tell she's smiling at me. She then puts rubber gloves on my Daddy. He plunges his right hand into the glove deeply and then it makes a snap sound on his forearm. And then the same thing happens with the left. And then it's my turn. With the nurse's help, I am successful. We walk about 4 feet to arrive at the side of the patient. The patient is already deeply asleep from the anesthesia and the skin is already prepped for incision. Evidently, there's been a lot going on here while we were at home chomping on Mama's biscuits and grits. My Daddy says "Scalpel", and a nurse shows him a tray of knives he can choose to use. I could really use that long one while fishing. He chooses one and begins his work. He makes a long incision across the abdomen, about 7 inches in length. The nurses on the other side are quickly cleaning up the initial blood. My dad works very purposeful and without hesitation. When he commands for an instrument, like a clamp, the nurse doesn't just hand it to him, she almost slams it into his hand so he can feel it. His hand is away, but his eyes never leave the spot where he is about to work.

He moves part of the patient's insides around to get to where he wants. He gets there, does some cutting of tissue, and then asks the nurse for some "cat gut." Apparently, the nurse read his mind, and hands him a half moon shaped needle attached to thick black thread. I really hope this thread wasn't made from cat guts. With some long clamps, he grabs the needle and starts sewing the insides of this person. He then speaks to me, "Boy, this black thread will dissolve inside his body in about a month after the tissues have grown back together." He then hands me a pair of scissors. I accept them in my left hand because I am left handed. In this right handed world, left- handers learn quickly how to cut with right handed scissors. Now I am in familiar territory. I have cut sutures for him in the Emergency Room many times. As my dad starts to finish, the nurses are cleaning away all the mess my Daddy made. He tells me to move closer to him. With clamps, he widely opens the the incision he made on the skin's surface. He then tells me and points to all the visible organs.

Everything is bright pink. He purposefully lifts the upper cut so I can see the base of the patient's lungs, and watch them work, expanding and contracting. But something is different about these lungs when compared to all the other things I saw inside. These lungs were not pink, they were an ugly light gray. They looked dirty. When my dad noticed what I just noticed, he said, "This man smokes cigarettes". That sight immediately cured me of any curiosity I may ever have about trying a cigarette. We then start closing the incision on the skin. I cut those sutures for him, too. While we are sewing, the person in charge of giving the anesthesia is sitting at the patient's head talking about how well the New York Yankees are doing right now. Mickey Mantle has just broken his previous home run record.

We finish up the last stitch and my dad says we have no more surgeries for today, like I was eager to start another one. Yeah, right. I am exhausted. It's now 12:45. We change into our street clothes and head home for dinner. We are both hungry. Willie Mae has fixed us her fried chicken, green beans, and smashed potatoes. We sit at the table in the den, with my dad sitting by the wall where there is a telephone mounted on the wall. During dinner, all of us are used to him picking up the phone, listening, and then asking the caller "How long have you had this diarrhea?" That was no "biggie" for us at the dinner table.

After Dinner, Mama and Daddy sit in front of the TV and watch their favorite TV soap opera, "As the World Turns." Mama is more into it than him. He really thinks it's stupid but watches it because she does. He then drifts into his daily nap until 2:45, then automatically wakes up. It's more predictable than the sun rising in the east. Mama has already taken Willie Mae home and starts puttering around the house and then leaves. One never knows what that woman can dream up in one afternoon.

So, Daddy's back at work, Mama's out doing something, and I'm right back where I began, watching the 3 Stooges on TV.

Bouncing in a soft gallop, my middle sister Maggie comes to me, "Want to come with me swimming?" I must be living right. This is great. I put on my swimming suit and yell to her, "I'm in the hot car waiting!" as if I can hurry her up. She finally comes, and we leave.

My Daddy is good friends with the mayor of West Point, Barnes Marshall, who owns Marshall Motel. It has a small but nice pool and he has told Daddy we may use it any time. We go there today because Maggie has a date with a new guy named Mark and wants to sun bathe. But on the way there she makes it really clear she did NOT want her hair to get wet. I mean, what's the point of going swimming if you don't want to get your hair wet? Destiny steps in. I had no choice but to do a giant "cannonball" off the diving board, and the splash soaking her head. As expected, she is furious with me and goes into a different version of how I was adopted and not really a member of the family. By now, I had figured it out and laughed until I cried. That was so much fun, just watching the smoke come from both her nostrils and both her ears. I could picture it as if I was watching a cartoon of "Wylie Coyote" chasing the ever elusive "Road Runner." To myself, I whispered, "Beep, beep."

We left the pool earlier because of two reasons: 1. A summer storm was in the brew, and 2. She now required more time to "do" her hair.

A brewing thunderstorm is now approaching a full boil. I briefly think about going fishing. I have caught more fish in the rain than not, but it was a passing thought. I had been wet and clean enough today.

Suppertime is near, according to my stomach. Mama is back now and tells me she had a bigger than normal choir practice tonight. She's the director and they are preparing for something big. She gets some cheddar cheese along with some crackers and calls that her supper. That would hardly fill up a bird.

Now I start figuring out the current situation. Mama is going out. Sister Maggie is going out. Daddy is not yet home. That means I get to cook, because I know better than to eat something Daddy cooks. Once, I said ONCE, I ate some "mystery" supper he fixed. I could not leave the bathroom for 3 days while experiencing propulsion comparable to that of a rocket coming from every orifice in my body. I learned my lesson well. The sad part is that I had been warned by both my sisters.

At 6:20, it was just me at the house. I looked inside the refrigerator and knew instantly where Mama had mysteriously gone. She had been to the Kwik Shop, a small local grocery, and re-stocked the refrigerator. Our favorite meat butcher, Gene, had cut us some fresh rib eye steaks, our favorite. Daddy specifically tells him to cut our steaks 1 1/4 inches thick, and he does so every time. The wind and the rain are no match for me. I was going to cook these beauties outside. That's the only place to cook a good steak. I went onto the back patio, grabbed an umbrella, and headed for the covered fire pit. Fella, my faithful dog, was at my side. One hand was holding the umbrella, and the other busily building the fire. That didn't take too long, so I didn't get too wet. While I was outside, Daddy got home. He greeted me, and asked, "What do you want me to cook for us?"

I quickly responded, "That's OK, I have it covered— we're having rib eyes and baked potatoes." He liked that idea. My stomach and my bowels clearly liked that idea. Earlier I had put the potatoes in the oven so the skin would get really good and crispy. I checked a little later, and the fire was almost ready. Daddy was seated in his recliner watching the news on TV, hosted by Walter Cronkite. President Johnson is talking about sending more troops into some far away place called Viet Nam. I don't know where that is. My Daddy is a man of few words, at times. He simply shook his head and said, "That war is not winnable." OK, he said that and he's my hero, so now that's what I think.

The rain has picked up and is now coming down really hard. As I said, the rain is no match for me. I sprinkle seasoning on the steaks, take them outside, grab my umbrella, and head for the fire. My dog, a full grown male German Shepard, perks up, smelling the meat. He follows me closely. I put the steaks on the grill and open the hood, so the flame will rise and sear the meat locking in the juices. I return to join my dad watching Uncle Walter and the news. Both Daddy and I can see the fire pit from the den. In a moment of sheer coincidence, we both see Fella raise up his paws to the hot pit and with his mouth grabs one of the steaks from the fire and runs away to get under cover with his prize. For a moment, both of us were speechless. Then my dad starts laughing, and that alone makes me laugh because his whole body wiggles when he laughs. He then says, "If Fella worked that hard to pull that steak out of the fire with a charred mouth and charred paws, then he deserves it." I agreed, and we had a big chuckle saying all the boys in the family were having steak tonight. So, I pull another one from the fridge, put it on, and we did some fine eating, of course, with ketchup.

And, as Walter Cronkite would say, "That's the way it is on this Summer day in 1967."

###Author's present day comment: 1)Laugh really hard with someone who is so comfortable in their own skin they can laugh equally as hard, 2) Precision is vital in some areas, but not others, 3)Laughing is more fun when you are laughing with someone with whom you care deeply.

Chapter 10
"Moonshine"
Age 13

It was forbidden for me to go deep into the woods hunting by myself. I had enough sense at this age of 13 to obey that. That in itself was a rarity.

I don't have my driver's license yet, but Mama lets me drive sometimes anyway.

The previous night of this encounter, Friday night, found me calling a few friends to squirrel hunt with me the next morning. Paul wanted to sleep in, Dave had a basketball game, and Michael Murphree was on that same team, so I didn't even call him. However, a beautiful spring day was being birthed and I was excited to go......any way I could figure out. Inside myself, I knew that squirrel hunting was better with two people because those little rascals are wily, and a little smart. When a squirrel sees you, he immediately goes to the other side of the tree. There are better results with two people.

However, rationalization and justification are wonderful things. They can be used in so many ways to bolster one's cause.

Fella, my German Shepard, was asked if he was willing to accompany me hunting the next morning. He anxiously said "yes." So, technically speaking, I was NOT going hunting by myself. I was accompanied by my trusty dog.

Squirrels are found in high trees, not low branches. That's where their nests are. Really, really high. And the nests are fairly big, too. They are much bigger than a bird's nest. They are not easily seen for two reasons, they are hidden behind branches, and that they are very high. Fella caught the scent of a squirrel and I encouraged him to go after it with my hand signal. He fled forward. A few minutes later, I saw one lone squirrel leaping from one high branch to another. Fella and I were now were on the same path. We were partners in high pursuit of those evil squirrels.

Then another was sighted, so I knew then the odds had instantly shifted to my favor. They kept leaping from one high branch to another, taking us deeper and deeper into the woods. I knew these woods, but I had not gone this deep into them before. I knew my directions based on moss only growing on the north side of a tree. And I knew the car was due east, so I was not the least concerned of getting lost. In reality, I had multitudes of guardian angels protecting me, because I was about to be in real danger.

As I followed sight and Fella followed scent, I started to smell something unfamiliar. It was a sweet smell, and a burning smell. It was not a good smell, just distinct. As I walked toward the smell, I began to see a stack of something, but could not make out what it was. I softly walked closer, rifle in hand. Now I could see the whole thing. Those stacks were stacks of corn, and that burnt smell was the smell coming out of a whiskey still which was in full operation. A deep sense of fear came over me, and chills, because I knew if I was found, my life would be in severe jeopardy. I grabbed Fella by the knap of the neck and we hit the ground. I was in the presence of a fully operational distillery, which I knew was extremely illegal. This still was powered by wood that was burning. The fire was hot, smoldering under a big jug. It then sent stuff up over a tube and then over some coils and then the liquid dripped down into a vat, and I remember seeing at the bottom of the vat some sort of outlet that you could twist, like a spout, to get liquid out of the vat. And I saw several cups by the spout. And I saw a couple of stools there, knocked over. I felt the palms of my hands getting sweaty on my rifle.

I felt that I was probably was the only one who stumbled across it. It was well enough off the beaten track that it was possible people never ran into it. I had just followed a squirrel from tree to tree to this point. And it was very portable. It was small enough and on wheels. It could have been in the back of a covered pickup. It was on sleds really, not wheels. It could be dragged.

I had some quick analyzing to do. The fire was burning, so I knew somebody was not really far away. I also knew that those people did NOT want me there under any circumstances. I also knew they would have guns. And I also knew they probably were drunk, and if I surprised or startled someone, shots would go everywhere, not just aimed at me. OK, then I thought of my favorite movies, Butch Cassidy and the Sundance Kid. In one scene, Butch said, "Never run out of options". I held on that sentence then, just as a parent would embrace a lost child.

Going backwards in the exact path we had taken was my only option. Then, I knew I could not let Fella run ahead or behind me, because he could accidentally cause a catastrophe. So, I kept close hold of his choke collar. We had him on a choke collar so that we had more control on him when he was around people he didn't know. I pulled the choke collar tight, and gently started to walk the opposite way. It was Spring, so there were not crumpling leaves under our feet. Fella was not a big barker, so I was not really concerned of his barking if we encountered squirrels on the way back.

That trip back seemed to take forever. My steps seemed like baby steps. My back started to hurt because I was couched over. Fella did not understand, but was totally obedient, somehow having a sense that something just was not right. Thank God we did not see any squirrels on the way back. Evidently, they had all moved far away from us upon our entry. That was an unexpected blessing.

I started to see familiar territory. I started to see the marsh from Tibbee Lake. I knew I was getting closer and closer. But it just felt like we were moving at a snail's pace.

In just a few moments, I could see the edge of the woods, and then I could see the car. Boy, what a relief!

We quietly got back in the car. We were on a slope. I wanted to get away, but I did not want the car to be heard. I put the car into neutral, and coasted down the road a bit. It was really hard to steer because the power steering was not on because the engine wasn't running. Then it was time to start the car.

While in neutral, I turned the switch, and the motor started. I then put it into drive. I did not wait for anything. I got away from there as quickly as possible.

It was mid-morning. As I drove closer to town, I thought, "I have to tell someone." But who? I knew I did not want to tell my Daddy. I could not tell him because I'd get too many lectures. As I got into my teen years, those lectures became somewhat of an annoyance because my Daddy's long talks got longer and deeper. Sometimes they were okay, and other times they were really an annoyance. OK, so who else? I thought, I could tell Paul. So, I did. And of all things, he laughed. Not what I expected at all. He told me the reason he laughed is because he had an uncle who ran a boot-leg liquor business in another town in Mississippi. In addition, he told me some inside information. He said I must have gotten so far into the woods that I was actually very close to the county line. He said that bootleggers put their stills next to the county line to restrict county law enforcement from going across county lines.

A few weeks later, my family was eating at the local restaurant, Mize's. I saw something then that I had hoped I would never see again.

I saw that still as FBI confiscated material in the restaurant, put on display. It was there—I know it was the very one—put on display as something unusual, of interest to people in restaurant. Just for observation.

But I didn't find it amusing at all.

###Author's present day reflections: 1) Manipulation is not a good thing 2) Manipulation can take me places I should not be going, 3)Learn quickly to make the best of a bad situation, 4) Sometimes, being fearful is smart, 5)How could this situation have been avoided?

Chapter 11
"The Unlikely Killer"
Age 14

Of all the adventures, mishaps, and just plain fun, there was only one time that I knew for sure my dog, Fella, might die. And it would not be as a result of being hit by a car, or a sharp and swift kick from an angry horse, it would be from the smarts of a small animal. An animal much smaller than my dog, but I knew something about that animal that my dog did not.

We, meaning my dog and me, are deep in the woods, this time hunting for rabbits. It is just beginning to turn seasons into fall, so the wind is sharp at times. Rabbits are plentiful because of their reproductive appetite, and also they know how to hide themselves and also to be really still....really still.

Can't we remember from our nursery tales of Uncle Remus, Tar Baby, and Burr Rabbit? In the fable, Burr Rabbit had been captured by an evil foe, and started pleading for his life by screaming, "PLEASE, PLEASE, just DON'T throw me into that thar briar patch!!"

In reality, the author of that story was telling the audience that the cunning rabbit was actually pleading with his foe to throw him into the briar patch, because that is by far the safest place for him to be.

Rabbits are basically nocturnal, meaning they like to do all their damage during the night and early morning.

But in the day, especially mornings, they can be flushed out with knowing just where to look, in and around briar patches.

Bear in mind these are marshy woods, simply because we are close to the edge of the Tombigbee River. And the water is beginning to get colder because of the change of the season. There are small pools of water all around containing small things like tadpoles and mosquitoes, and bigger and badder things like water moccasins, who move slower now because of the colder temperatures. But they have not completely disappeared. And they can still kill me.

Speaking of snakes, I don't fear them. My Daddy taught me that. But I do respect them and what damage they can do if I cross their boundary. But with that high mindedness thinking, they are so much fun to kill. And I keep reminding myself, has one ever known a happy ending to a story involving an encounter with a snake? So I felt a certain duty to do my share. My .22 caliber Remington rifle my dad gave me on my 10th birthday is a faithful ally.

But today was not that type of encounter. Today is different. Much different. In our pouncing through the woods, we disturb a mama raccoon. Bad idea. Bad situation. Bad everything. Nothing good can come can come from this, I thought, especially if she has a cub hidden nearby. I would have preferred to upset a mama bobcat, no question about that.

As I suspected, as soon as Fella knew this was not a rabbit, but a raccoon, he gets excited, really excited. He badly wants that raccoon in his mouth. Instantly, he turns in that direction and runs full speed, and so do I, but for a much different reason. I can feel the cold soggy soil beneath my feet allowing my feet to sink deeper into the soil. My feet sinking deeper allows river smells to emerge. I feel my heart pounding, not only from my own physical exertion, but from the eminent danger present.

I know what is REALLY happening. That mama raccoon is drawing us nearer and nearer to a pool of water. It is a planned evil plot.

Those who spend a good amount of time in the woods know that a raccoon does not have glands which produce saliva. They have to be around water when they eat. They have to dip their food into a bit of water, giving it moisture in order for them to swallow.

But it is not the intent of that raccoon that my dog become her dinner, rather the mission of that raccoon is for Fella to be her latest victim. How could this possibly be?

Raccoons are excellent swimmers, much better than dogs. They lure dogs into the middle of a pond, and then, in a split second, change roles from victim to murderer. The dog almost has the raccoon in its mouth, and then the raccoon makes the move. They actually climb upon the dog's head, and then push the dog's nozzle into the water, thus drowning the dog.

I am screaming for Fella to stop, screaming over and over, "STOP!" But he is excited. He makes it to the edge of the water pool before I do, and then he hesitates. Labrador retrievers would not have hesitated at all; rather they would have leaped into the water because that's what they were made to do. But Fella was a German Shepard, a guard dog.

When he hesitated, I make my move. I drop my rifle, run toward him with fleeting thoughts of carrying home a dead dog, and then lunge face forward; arms outstretched into the cold water, and am able to grab a hind foot. I hold on as tightly as I can, with him trying to pull away and pursue. I am wet, cold, my gun is wet, but I have a foot in my hand. And that was enough.

The raccoon was already in the middle of the pond, swimming in a circle, waiting. But Fella is now in my arms, safe from an unknown murderer.

After I calm down my dog, I can breathe easier. I escort Fella away from that scene as quickly as possible.

Minutes later, we are away and after another adventure.

Little did Fella know that this was the day I saved his life.

During the cold ride home, I thought about the morning's events. After I get home, I am hungry and smell Willie Mae cooking fried chicken. I begin cleaning my rifle to get the river gunk out of it. I then think of one of the Dirty Harry movies, like Dirty Harry XVI, and Clint Eastwood had just cornered his greatest foe. The foe was asking himself, "did he shoot 5 times at me, or 6"? Dirty Harry confirmed his thought.

Then he said to the bad guy, "A man's got to know his limitations". And then Harry clicked his 6 shooter revolver and shot the bad guy dead.

Today, that statement did not apply to me. Not this day. I loved my dog. I was willing to do anything to save him….. from himself.

A couple of weeks later, I was in Church with my dad listening to Rev. Dinas preach. His message was Jacob wrestling with God. And listening to Rev. Dinas tell that story, it was quite a wrestling match. And a foot was grabbed. But that was enough.

In some sorted way, I knew. And that was enough.

####Author's present day comment: 1) Wolves in sheep's clothing are all around, 2) Common sense is a good thing.

Chapter 12
"The White Cloud in my Face"
Age 15

This misadventure had to have happened on a Wednesday, because my mother asked me to drive her to Columbus, a nearby larger town, to do a little shopping at her favorite small store, Lagniappe, which is French for "a little something extra", owned and operated by a dear friend, Betty Clyde. She had just returned from the beauty shop called "Lois's, named for her good friend, Lois Kisner. And that event occurred every Wednesday at 1:30, right after taking Willie Mae home.

So it was about 3 pm when she and I started to Columbus. We went in what was known as "her car", a late model Buick Electra 225. It really drove nicely, but she always wanted to drive a Cadillac, but Daddy just did not see that, even though he absolutely adores her. We had an unusual driveway. It was made from sea shells. Daddy, the eccentric, had two big trucks full of seashells drive from the Mississippi Gulf Coast to dump them in our driveway. They are beautiful. They are brilliant white. That new driveway smelled of the sea and was hard to look at in the bright sunshine because they reflected the light. We backed out of the driveway, turned at the corner, and then made one more turn at Mr. Ward's Country Store. Mama gladly honored my request to stop at Ward's and get me a frozen chocolate fudge bar. Then we were on our way to what I thought would be a routine trip to Columbus.

WOW! Was that ever an untrue statement! The ride out of town was on Mississippi HWY 50 East, toward the Alabama border. We passed a few familiar businesses, all of which knew us and waved. We were the family of "Dr. R.B." The speed limit was 65 and it was an overcast day in summer, and the humidity was high, so things were sticky.

The trek to Columbus usually takes about 25 minutes. About 12 minutes into it, we pass a huge curve, maybe 2 miles in length. On both sides I see beautiful crops of soybeans, milo, and corn. That scene has always been beautiful to see and I look forward to it every time. The crops grow well there because they benefit from being in the small delta from the nearby Tombigbee River. The soil is rich with nutrients making the soil black as coal. This location is about 3 miles from the River, and close to the rail trussell, which is one of my favorite playgrounds.

But before we got to the end of the giant curve, we come upon an unusual truck, moving much slower than us. It was a chicken truck. It was the biggest chicken truck I had ever seen, and it was carrying tens of thousands of chickens. These were bright white chickens, not the brown barnyard type. And they were headed for market.

But something was about to happen which would score my memory.

The truck was traveling slower simply because of the weight involved, so I slowed down. And this truck was high, so there was a wall of chickens right in front of us, each one of them staring right at us.

I asked my Mama, "Do you feel like a monkey in the zoo"? She laughed, and then said, "I wonder what all those chickens are thinking right now?" I responded, "I bet they hope they are headed to Columbus to shop with you at Lagniappe." She laughed. She is so easy to make laugh. She is my best audience. She always "accepted" me in all circumstances, especially since I had sensitive feelings, and my mean sisters would call me "Raygene" when I was hurt. She always took up for me.

Then, in a nan a-second, things began to radically change. It seems everything went into slow motion. Instead of me looking for an opportunity to pass him on this two lane highway, I instantly saw a lone chicken jarred away from the truck and he was floating head first right into my windshield! He had sheer terror in his beady eyes. And instantly after that, I felt a minor thump on my windshield, and then what seemed like hundreds of thousands of bright white feathers were right in front of me surrounding my windshield! I could still make out the road, so I felt no danger. And then laughter took me over completely, and my mother completely lost it laughing. We were both laughing so hard, tears were coming down both our faces.

It was like, that chicken was there one moment, and then, POOF! He became a cloud of feathers!

It took us a few moments to regain composure, but this chicken truck was still traveling in front of us, totally oblivious to what we had just experienced nor what was about to happen.

As I mentioned earlier, the truck was very high. One must be aware that the Mississippi highways are not famous for being the smoothest in the nation. The tax base simply is not there. There are potholes. And I knew everyone of them, because this was familiar territory to me. I knew this driver's problems were far from over.

Two seconds after that thought, things fell apart really fast.

The driver hit a known pothole and that truck began to tip to the right. I told Mama, "Watch this". Then, as if it were in slow motion again, that whole chicken truck was gently falling over to the right. On the way down, the wire cages broke, and thousands upon thousands of chickens unexpectedly became airborne. And, chickens can't fly, but they did that day!

As these thousands of chickens were forced from the comforts of their coops, their circumstances instantly changed in such a way that they were forced to open their wings.......and FLOAT down! It was a sight I will never forget. I am quite confident my mouth was stuck wide open and saliva was dripping from my face. It not a cool thing to do for a 16 year old kid to drool in front of his mother. However, there were some girls at the pool which had the same affect on me. Anyway, the huge brilliant white cloud of chickens gently floated to the ground, safe from harm.

The thought never entered my mind as to what those chickens would do upon their descent to earth. It was like a thirteen ring circus in motion! I stopped the car. I could not get this type of entertainment in the movies! This was way beyond hysterically funny. My mother and I were beyond words. Our expressions of amazement were enough. And the laughter described earlier paled in comparison to what we were witnessing now! We saw thousands upon thousands of white chickens running aimlessly in and out of soybean rows.

I would call this "Chaos Exponential 10X!"

Never before have I seen anything like this, and certainly not since.

The driver of the truck and his helper got out of the truck and just threw up their hands in disbelief. They were absolutely helpless in the hopes of putting any part of this puzzle back together.

I thought about what are these poor guys going to say to their bosses? How could they explain this at all?

After a bit of time, Mama and I continued our trek to Columbus, but constantly talking about the incident. The necessary, or should I say, desired shopping was successful.

On the way home, we saw a few straggler chickens wandering around. I told Mama, "I think I will take one home for fun." She just said keep it outside. I agreed. I stopped the car and chased one down and put it in the trunk.

When I got home, I immediately called Paul to tell him what had happened. He said he would be over in five minutes. I did not know why. When he arrived he asked, "Where's the chicken?" I took him outside. He reached out, picked up that chicken, and said, "I can make this chicken drunk." I laughed and said OK. He then put the chicken's head under its wing, and then twirled around a few times. When the chicken was let go, it ran around as if it had just finished a pint of Jack Daniels sour mash whiskey.

This had been a really fun day.

###Author's present day comment:1)Be observant, 2)Find a reason to laugh, 3)Who says chickens can't fly?

Chapter 13
"Intentional prejudice" Age 15

For the last two weeks, in English Class, we have been studying Oliver Swift's, *Gulliver's Travels*. Swift used a massive amount of satire of the English throne, government, and people. I am enjoying it because I love clever satire, and this is certainly one of those.

In the book, Gulliver encounters the Lilliputians. The Lilliputians are men six inches in height but possessing all the pretension and self-importance of full-sized men. They are mean and nasty, vicious, morally corrupt, hypocritical and deceitful, jealous and envious, filled with greed and ingratitude — they are, in fact, completely human. Also, in the book, the little people go to war over such things as whether or not to use butter or syrup on pancakes.

I am 15 years old. Even I, a youngster, can clearly see the absurdity of the story. It is utterly ridiculous, and inhumane. And so is racism.

One of the duties and responsibilities I have now that I have my driver's license is to go get Willie Mae, our cook and helper. It's a crisp autumn morning. I travel from our street, Broad Street, over to McCord. I then take a right onto McCord Street, and then a left onto Main Street. I see many big oaks losing beautiful, colorful leaves. The leaves are in the street. That route is the only route to her house where I don't have to go through a less than safe area. When I was younger, my mama would call a morning like this a "Blue Horse" morning. That meant it was fall and time to go to the store and get me a tablet for writing that happened to have a blue horse on the cover.

So, today qualifies as a "Blue Horse" morning. It is absolutely clear, very few high clouds, and cold.

As I turn right headed for her house, I come to a 4 way stop intersection. I stop. On my left I see the business of Alvin Carter, a friend of mine and my family's. He runs a black ambulance/funeral business, as did his father. He is a natural leader and has a fine reputation in town. On the right, I see an open field, an empty field, but not totally empty today. I see 3 wooden cross still burning, still smoldering from a blaze which occurred a few hours earlier. I don't move. I absorb what I was seeing.

I could only imagine what hatred those cowardly men had for themselves in order to lower themselves to join an organization which promotes their own race as "the chosen," and other races of people are inherently inferior. The irony is they even chose to hide their identity with white capes, and white hats, and in this era, rode in trucks rather than on horseback, as did the previous generations of extremists. My friend, Alvin Carter, whose skin happens to be black, was their target a couple of hours earlier. As I lingered at the intersection, I saw Alvin's car, knowing he was at home. He looked out the window, and seeing that it was me, he came out. I pulled into his driveway and got out. He immediately started describing the horror. He had the look of a terrorized child. He explained how his family was harassed, windows in his home broken by bricks, and the yelling of obscenities and hatred. I felt so sorry for him. I felt so sorry for his precious family. He has a daughter just a year behind me in school. I felt so sorry for her. The pain they endured is the worse kind.....when it's intentional. It is so not right. I kept telling Alvin, "it's not about you", "it's not about you!" In his justifiable anger, he responded; "Ray, what would you have me feel right now?"

I was stunned. I was set back. I thought for what seemed like an hour, and I said to him, "Alvin, you should feel pity on those cowards". He broke into tears and said, "Ray, it's hard to do that right now because I know the only reason they did this is because I have black skin." I totally understood. I really could not comprehend his pain at that moment. At that moment, I was embarrassed for my own race. Olivia, Alvin's beautiful wife, came out. She obviously saw Alvin speaking with me, and came out. We hugged, as we normally do, and I expressed my sorrow, not for what they have endured, not just contained to what had happened in the last few hours, but for the prejudice they have felt and experienced for so long simply because Alvin is a natural leader of men, and runs a successful business.

My relationship with Alvin in those moments went to level 7 on the depth scale. From that experience onward, when we greeted one another, we both reached out our arms and hugged one another.

As the 3 of us were regaining our composure, it was almost 9:30 and I knew mama would be wondering what was going on. So, I get back in the car, and head for Willie Mae's house. When I get to that yellow house, which I painted last summer, I continued 100 yards or so, to the next intersection. I turned around, as my mama does, so that Willie Mae is on the passenger side. She got into the back seat, as she continually chose to do, against my wishes. We said our hellos. And then, I thought of another route I could take back to the house. So I turned right at the next intersection instead of going straight. She broke the silence. She asked me why I was going this way instead of the normal way. I responded,

"There's road work on the other road". She spoke quickly, "I know what happened" in her soft spoken manner. I could not phantom what was going through her mind in that moment. She is a very wise woman, in a very simple way. The remark she made seared into my very being. "Ray, some people just don't like us colored people 'cause our skin is a different color."

On the inside, I was shattered. I was undone. My precious Willie Mae, just as much of my own family as I, was speaking a truth which had to be let loose. She expressed a truth which was "unspeakable."

The Civil Rights Act was passed when I was 11 years old. My family, and most people, knew that it was, fundamentally, a good and righteous thing. The paradox remained. The people whose skin was black did not want to go to school with us whites, nor did the whites desire to go to school with the blacks.

Nevertheless, the mandate from the federal government was to integrate. I'm in high school. OK, great, so to where do we integrate? There are not schools big enough to house us all, so the solution was to go to school in shifts. One group went to school from 7:30 to 1pm, and the other group went from 1:30 to 6. It was not effective. The government did not receive the desired result.

The intent is recognized. All this chaos, because of the color of one person's skin?

Get real. Sounds too much like the Lilliputians.

###Author's present day comment: 1)Nothing good comes from any type of racism, 2)Learn to think quickly on how to help someone in a tight situation.

Chapter 14
A DESTINY WITH LIGHTNING
Age 15

Last night, my night-owl Daddy and I were up late watching "The Tonight Show" with Johnny Carson. My Daddy does not think Carson is so funny, but I enjoy him sometimes. Since I am at home, I see Daddy put down his mystery novel he had begun reading earlier in the evening. Carson is doing his monolog, as he normally does. During the monolog, he brings up how hot it is in "Beautiful Downtown Burbank," (which he hates). He says the people in Burbank say, "It's a 115 degrees, but it's a DRY heat. Carson then explodes in laughter, yelling "It's 115 DEGREES! YOU COULD FRY YOUR ENTIRE MEALS ON YOUR ROOF!" The in-studio audience roars. At that, I start laughing, and I see my Daddy chuckle. He's not a loud laughing person, but a coveted moment is when he gets really tickled at something, he can't stop laughing, and watching that alone is extremely funny.

The reason I am intrigued with Carson's remarks regarding the heat is because it's mid-summertime here in Mississippi. That means high temperatures combined with high humidity, and the result is pure misery. I spend a lot of time outdoors, so at least two showers a day are common practice. The weather outside feels like we live in a hot sauna. There should be a natural law prohibiting such a weather mix. I'll have to speak to the proper authorities about that. People move slower and stay more indoors. Boy, do I wish I had been the person to invent air conditioning.

Daddy knows how much I like to fish. He likes to order things out of catalogs he gets in the mail. Because of me, we subscribe to a magazine called Field and Stream. Late yesterday, a package arrived at the house addressed to Daddy. It went without notice until he got home from the clinic. After supper, he picks up the mysterious package and calls "K' mere, boy."

On my way to honor his request I ponder why they gave me a name. Nobody uses it. I get to him and he hands me his prized pocket knife. He is a connoisseur of finely crafted pocket knives. I guess it goes along with being a surgeon. This is a black one, very slender, and has his initials, RBF, etched on the side. I open the longer of the two blades, but before I start to open the package, I check out the sharpness of the blade. It's like nothing I have. This knife would go through stone like a hot knife going through butter. I take a moment to press in re: the other contents of his pockets. He shows me, and I see in the left pocket the knife, lip balm, mints, a nail clipper. In the right pocket I find a money clip with a little folding money, which is interesting. He told me a laxative drug representative gave several of them to him in a recent visit. I look at it carefully, do a double-take, and start laughing. He instantly knows why I am laughing and got a big smile. It was the inscription on the money clip which was funny. It read: *"Laxation without procrastination or irritation wins patient cooperation."* He says he'll give me one of the extras. I jumped at that.

I open the box, and am immediately aghast! I am looking at a picture of a fisherman using a bizarre instrument to fish called a BAZOOKA FISH POLE. I am on the receiving end of this gift. My Daddy proudly opens the box and removes this thing. At the bottom, this thing has a trigger, and at the top is a small plastic cup to hold a fishing lure. From the top, the rod is like a telescope, having the capacity to to be pushed down upon itself with a spring collapsing inside. When it is pushed down far enough, it clicks and cocks the trigger. Daddy then describes that now the fisherman only points to where he wants the lure to go, and simply pulls the trigger, and like BAM, the rod come fully expanded, and the lure is hurled into the air, and supposedly lands where I want. Now, I am more able to understand why it's called the BAZOOKA FISH POLE. Yes, it does remind me of a bazooka gun which the Army uses. I thank him for this gift, and tell him I am going fishing tomorrow. He likes that.

On my way back to my bedroom, I'm thinking how much I dread the moment my friend Paul sees this thing. I'm going to wait until we get in Paul's car to show him, because I know loud he's going to laugh. Paul loves my Daddy like he loves his own, but knows my Daddy is an eccentric. This gift is simply another confirmation. Upon seeing it, as predicted, he gets tears in his eyes laughing. Then he does like he <u>always</u> does, he starts listing just a FEW of my dad's eccentric traits:

A. His obsession with extremely hot flavors. When we go to a Mexican restaurant, he gets the hottest peppers available. It is so funny to watch tears streaming down his while smiling broadly and saying "that's good stuff".

B. His reputation as a masterful sandwich maker in the wee hours of the morning. He goes to the grocery store by himself for these unique ingredients. Mama says he wakes up with "gorilla breath".

C. His liking to order things from the back of catalogs. It gives an entirely new meaning to the word "surprise". He once ordered a big hat for use while deep sea fishing in Destin, FL. It was so wide, nobody could get within several feet of him. He failed to see the humor.

D. His unique sense of humor. When he observes a dog chasing a car, he solemnly comments: "I wonder what magnificent plans that dog has for that car if he is so blessed to catch it?"

Paul calls me about 1pm and says Father Bob is joining us today for fishing. I laugh and say that's fine. Father Bob is older than us, in his mid-twenties, and is the Priest of this small Catholic Parish. The three of us have been together several times, mostly eating out on the eternal search to find the finest fried catfish "hole in the wall" restaurant.

Every time the three of us go out to eat, Father Bob breaks tradition. When we order, Father Bob asks the waitress to bring his dessert first while Paul and I are eating our salads. The first time I saw this, I was astonished, and asked him why he did this. His response was "If I die during supper, I want to be finished with my favorite part". The odd part is that since then the more I have given thought to that, the more sense it makes to me. Father Bob has 3 cats at his apartment. He named them Surely, Goodness, and Mercy. Why? Because they follow him everywhere. Anyway, he has never been fishing with us, so this should be interesting, at the very least.

My car is in the shop and so I get on my bike, which is behind the house, and I get on it and ride over to Paul's house around the corner. Paul is a year older than I, and has his license and a car, a Plymouth Duster. The boat we use is behind their house. We pick it up and mount it bottom up on top of the car and strap it down. The boat is about five feet longer than the car. It's a sight.

I really should take a picture.

We go to Father Bob's apartment complex to pick him up. Then we head for Walker's Lake. It's a private fishing lake located about five miles west of town. As we get out of town, we cross Sukatanchee Creek. It's named for a famous Chickasaw Indian. This was heavy Indian country. We look at the level of the creek, it's high, and that's a good sign. When it rises and over flows, a fun thing to do is to get rubber boots on and go there and gather "craw-daddys," which is a "want-to-be" shrimp. They are crayfish. They are great when boiled in a good shrimp boil. Then we put newspapers folded out on the floor and sit and eat until we can't eat anymore. But that's not for today.

We stop at Ward's Grocery Store on the way to the lake. We need some snacks, bait, stuff like that. One of my favorites is an RC Cola and a Moon Pie. That combo is awesome! But today I think I'll get a Butterfinger now and also get a Pay Day peanut bar for later in the day. The Pay Day won't melt like the chocolate. Paul and Father Bob get their treats, too. We also get some ice and put a few King Sized Cokes in the small cooler we bring.

On the drive out to the lake, Paul turns on the radio. He hunts around for something he wants to listen to. He finds his favorite, Simon and Garfunkel, singing their hit song, "Bridge Over Troubled Water". It happens to be one of my favorites as well. There's only one problem. Paul can't carry a tune in a bucket nor can Father Bob. I am absolutely dying listening to them. They are killing me. It's sacrilegious how bad they sound. I hope those cats of Father Bob's are tone deaf. No doubt a good dog would just leave and run away. Paul then says, "Ray, please sing with us, you are the only one who can keep us on pitch!" Unfortunate, but true. So I join in, reluctantly. So here we are, eating Butterfingers, drinking Cokes, singing to the top of our lungs, now on pitch, and laughing at the people staring at us because we have a boat tied on the top of the car. Ya know, when you're just "in the moment", nothing else matters.

We get to the lake, which is about twelve acres in size. It's great for catching bream, a "pan-fry" fish, crappie, and large mouth bass. Paul and I know the routine. We get to either end of the boat and lift it and take it to the water. We mount the small 10hp motor on one end, and then I have a small trolling motor which I mount on the opposite end.

It's about 3:30 now, and we put Father Bob in the middle section and push ourselves off. It's in the heat of the day, so we know the big bass have run deep for cooler water. So fishing for big bass is reserved for later in the day today.

The bream and crappie run in schools, and the best way to find them is to motor abound and look for activity on the surface. Our search today doesn't take long at all. Over toward the shore and overhanging branches is where wee see them feeding. My only reluctance in making haste is those overhanging branches. They sometimes contain snakes sunbathing. Snakes and I do not get along. It goes way back.

A few weeks ago, Paul and I were fishing here in another cove. We casually lumbered under some branches. I cast out my bait and the lure went into some branches instead. I was right at the branches. I raised up my rod and hit a branch, trying to dislodge my bait. What I didn't know I was that I didn't hit a branch at all. I hit a water moccasin and had just ruined his day. In like kind, I guess he thought he'd ruin mine as well. My rod actually knocked him off the branch, and gravity went into action, and he fell fell right into the middle of the boat, startled and really upset. Paul and I dropped out rods and immediately gave that serpent the boat. We jumped into the shallow water, which was about waist deep, and waited until that snake realized he liked water better than metal. He slivered over the side and we watched him crawl onto shore. Paul and I started laughing. If only this could have been on TV.

As we motor toward the activity on the surface, I mention that experience to Paul. He just laughed and said "today I have my pistol with rat shot". That was comforting to me. When we tell Father Bob that little episode, he now seems a little uneasy, a little unsettled. We both assure him we have things under control and that nobody would be forced to swim today. As Paul and Father Bob start to fish, I put down the anchor so we won't drift.

We all have Zebco rods and reels, although Paul's is a little longer than mine. I have always been fascinated with that company. They make great stuff for fishing. But that's not how they got famous. They got famous because they made the best bombs used in WW2. I guess somebody really smart at that company dreamed up the idea of making fishing stuff after the war. I think that's really cool.

On their first cast, they both catch a fish. Both are bream. Paul and I know we have hit pay dirt, pure gold. When they go into a feeding frenzy like this, one could throw a Coke can in the middle and they'd give a good shot at trying to eat it. Now, it's really getting fun. On every cast we make, we get a fish. I am in charge of the fish stringer at the other end of the boat, so Paul and Father Bob hand me their fish to be put on the stringer hanging over the boat. It's attached to the boat with an easy-off clamp, so it's easy for me to lift the stringer out of the water and find an empty metal hanger, string the fish through the mouth and gills, and then clamp. I then am able to drop the stringer back in the water to keep them alive.

All three of us have a license to fish. The Mississippi Game and Fish Commission regulates the population of the fish. We know that our daily limit on bream is 15 per rod. Sometimes we fish for catfish, and we'll have two or three rods each, because there's no limit. But that's not the case when catching bream. They keep you really busy.

It takes about a ½ hour for Paul and Father Bob to catch their limit. It takes me a little longer because the stringer is near me.

Then, yes, I get my limit too. The three of us are now bragging how well we have done and how we need to be on the cover of some national magazine for this phenomenal achievement. We are laughing, telling tall tales, and marveling at what we had done. The fish are still in a frenzy, apparently not aware that 45 of them were missing. We could have stayed there much longer, but saw no point to it. My hands are really smelly.

As Paul maneuvers to start the bigger motor, Father Bob asks me to lift the stringer once more to admire our booty. I gladly oblige. I pull the stringer up very slowly because its now quite heavy. What I saw next triggered all displacement of my intestines and my bladder! My eyes popped out of their sockets when I saw what was on our fish!

There was a snake wrapped around my beehive bundle of fish and he had his mouth clamped onto one of my fish! I don't know who was more startled, ME or that blasted snake! Paul is quick! He yells to me, "He's not a viper and he can't bite you, his mouth is busy and he now has no leverage!" I knew all that to be true, however, Paul was NOT the one holding that stringer! Paul yells again, "Shake him off, shake him off ! Who am I, Hercules, Superman, <u>MOSES</u>?" And what business of theirs to tell me what to do that serpent? That snake is not interested in <u>THEM</u>, he's furious at <u>ME</u>! OK, with excrement in my pants I start shaking the stringer, as if I'm not already shaking! Their feeble-minded plan does work. This snake loosens his mouth and drops back into the water. Paul and Father Bob are laughing hysterically AT me, not WITH me, and how shaken up I am. I take a few moments of private time to clean where necessary, and we move on.

It's about 5 or 5:30 now, and we know that the bass are beginning to surface looking for something to eat. Paul really wants his Priest to catch a bass, and I don't blame him. I wish there was some empathy for me, but no. We motor away from the shady shore a little ways and change out lures for bass.

Paul brings out a bass fishing lure he bought especially for Father Bob. He pulls it out of the box, I can see it's very shiny, and he hands it to me for my examination. I look at it very carefully. This thing looks almost identical to one of my mother's finest earrings, minus the hooks.

Paul ties his lure onto Father Bob's line just like I do. My Daddy taught us both a really cool surgical knot that never comes loose.

Father Bob is now poised to meet his destiny of catching a trophy bass. He's excited, sitting at the edge of his seat. He casts out really far and that lure stirs up the surface flapping and jiggling all the way back as Father Bob reels it in, trying to make it look like a wounded minnow, a favorite for bass. All 3 of us are fishing, each using a different technique. Paul is using a jig, which swims below the surface a little ways, enticing the bass with its back and forth movement. I am using a black plastic worm, imitating a "night crawler", about 8 inches long. I really like those because I can actually feel a bass playing with the worm before he chomps down on it. Father Bob is really into this and is not derailed after several unsuccessful casts. After about 10 minutes of us all fishing the same side of the boat, Father Bob announces "Somebody once said, 'Cast on the other side of the boat.'"

We all laughed and turned ourselves toward the other side. We all 3 cast out at the same time, and instantly,, a huge bass strikes at Father Bob's lure, and now his rod is now shaped like a half moon because of the weight. We tell him to give it a jerk to set the hook, and he does. Now the fight begins. I don't have the anchor down because there's no breeze and I can feel this bass actually moving the boat! I pull my worm in quickly so to help as necessary. Paul also reels his in and grabs the fishing net and positions himself closer to Father Bob, who is now completely engaged. Paul rightly tells him to tire the fish out, not to just quickly reel him in, knowing the line is likely to break if done so. So Father Bob reels him in a little ways, against the will of the fish. And then he eases the line to let the fish swim. We all hear the reel screaming as the fish goes deep trying to escape.

Father Bob is in control, seemingly. He's shaking a little, but that's just the "rush". He's certainly not shaking like I was earlier. The Priest had thrown this lure really far out, so there was some real estate to cover between the fish and us. As Father Bob gets this trophy closer, Paul reaches out with the net. It was not close enough. On the next "to-and-fro" cycle, Father Bob eases the line, and then the fish makes a final move for its life. It jumps out of the water, about 3 feet away from us, and shakes his head back and forth, and throws the lure out of its mouth and makes a big splash as he hits the water, getting us all 3 wet.

Now......there is deafening silence, and Father Bob's face is getting really, really, red. He stands up in the boat, putting us all in danger. He violently throws the rod and reel into the water and starts cursing everything and I do mean everything and everybody in the universe! The foul language coming from this mild mannered "man of the cloth" would embarrass a very drunken sailor in Singapore! This went on and on with no stopping! Paul and I looked at each other in silent desperation, knowing that if lightning could strike without a cloud in the sky, the time would be now and the place would be right here! And it's a METAL boat! We are ALL TOAST! We are cooked and can't escape! We will <u>fry</u> as a result of the lightning strike upon Father Bob!

Father Bob yells, "THAT WAS MY FISH! THAT WAS MY FISH!" We both eagerly agree with him, trying to coax him to sit down! We try to console this now sobbing Priest. Not just a gentle cry, but wailing loudly in the agony of defeat. Paul and I felt so sorry for him we did not know what to do or say.

Fortunately, the rod he threw into the water was made with a cork handle, so it wasn't hard to find. Paul pulled it back into the boat, and the famous lure was still attached. I think to myself, "what a good knot that is". Paul and I suggest we have had enough for today. Father Bob reluctantly agreed. We promised we'd bring him back soon to catch HIS fish. Paul and I are prepared to burn a little because we both intend NOT to bring him out again. We both love him, but the odds of lightning striking are increasing moment by moment.

We motor over to the landing and Paul goes to get the car. We lift the boat onto the top and strap it down tight. I get in the back seat so Father Bob can sit up front. There's not too much talking on the way back into town. I guess it just seemed to me enough had already been said. We drop Father Bob off at his apartment while seeing Surely, Goodness, and Mercy waiting for him in the window. Paul says, "See you at Mass." I chuckle only to myself.

We go to Paul's house because unloading the boat is a two man job. I help him unload and he remarks, "Sundance, why can't we just have a normal day of fishing, like everybody else?" (He always calls me that and I call him Butch, a takeoff of the movie "Butch Cassidy and the Sundance Kid"). I respond, "Butch, but would that be as much fun as we have?" He laughingly answers "No, Sundance."

We put all those fish we caught in Paul's outside refrigerator and take vows to clean them in the morning.

My house is just around the corner from Paul's. It's about 7:30pm. I hop onto my bike, but before pedaling, I put my smallest two fingers in my mouth and let out a loud whistle, to signal my dog, Fella, that I was on my way. Then I start home. And sure enough, there he is, running toward me, eager to see me. He smells the fish odor on my hands as I pet him, and we're almost home.

Mama and Daddy are there and Daddy wants to hear about "BAZOOKA FISH POLE". I say, "I'm exhausted...... just smell my fingers". That was good enough for him, so that's just good enough for me, too.

###Author's present day comment: 1)Recognize the little things...sometimes you'll find a pearl, 2) Protect the feelings of others, 3)Knowing the difference between real danger, and laughing fearlessly, 4) People can be really surprising in their behavior.

Chapter 15
age 16
"Stuff it with gauze"

The Saturday nights I spend in the emergency room accompanying Daddy seem countless. It is my way of just getting to be with him. Going with him when called upon to pull out a bullet, or clean and stitch a knife wound, or re-assemble a man's abdomen as a result of a knife fight, delivering a baby, are the norm for me. They are the best way I know I can be with my dad, simply because he is so busy.

Bear in mind that these years I spend with him in the ER are in my teen years. The care I consistently see being given to these suffering people has been and remains without comparison.

Sometimes volumes of information can be transferred without the utterance of a syllable. And much less a word, less even a detestable sentence.

Such is this event one Saturday night.

It was a slow Saturday night in comparison to the sheer quantity of calls normally. Earlier in the evening we pulled a .38 caliber lead cartridge from a man's leg, cleaned it, stitched it, put disinfectant on it, and sent him on his way.

Good thing it was a .38 caliber cartridge, commonly used for target practice. Had it been a .38 hollow point, the procedure would have taken on an entirely different face. A hollow point in a bullet implodes upon impact, creating a "mushroom" effect. It it very, very lethal.

But it was later in the evening when it got interesting, really interesting.

A young woman, in her teens, was brought into the ER on a stretcher. She had been involved in an automobile accident and sustained a really messed up knee. The wound was open, flesh torn from flesh, and exposed bone. But when she was being rolled in, the screaming of obscenities were simply outrageous. This person's foul language including the taking of the Lord's name in vain was permeating the entire room, a small emergency room. I thought to myself that we should throw a little dirt into her wound to match her mouth. My dad worked on her knee as if the rest of her was not in the room. Silently, he worked. This was unusual, because he was normally telling me what to do, like "boy, hold the suture right here", or "press your fingers here to help stop the bleeding." No, not now. Not at this moment. With just a glance, he simply motioned me to get more straps to hold her down. I did so…very quickly. But that action designed to help her actually enraged her with more viciousness. Again, I thought to myself, "How is he doing this?"

It was at that moment that I witnessed something very loud, something which I had never seen, or ever expect to again, without the utterance of a sound. He picked up his small clamps, and gathered six to ten 4X4 cotton gauze pads, and then with his other hand cut a 5 inch piece of tape. He then took the cotton gauze in the clamps, and put the gauze pads in her mouth, and then put tape over her mouth. The immediate silence was deafening. I mean, it was like coming out of a dark theater into broad daylight, where you have to give your eyes time to adjust.

If there was ever a moment where something should have been said, this would certainly have been it. But, no, not a word was spoken. My dad quickly got back to work, cleaning the automobile debris from her knee. He then was able to repair the torn muscles, repair the torn cartilage, then able to discover the kneecap was not fractured. He then, by himself, reattached the torn flesh to its proper place with stitches, without my help. After completing those tasks, he poured sulfur over the wounded area to avoid infection. Then he bandaged the knee completely, and inserted a brace.

After that, it was time for her, and us, to go home.

I, as I normally would do, got into the driver's seat. Driving him was usually one of my tasks. We were headed home. I could tell he was tired. But I didn't push conversation.

As I was turning into our driveway, he, in his soft voice, said, "Nobody takes my Lord's name in vain if I can help it."

It was then that I saw another dimension of my father.

Here was a man who was there to help. He was there to provide aid. And he did that valiantly. But that was part of his job. What wasn't his job was to put up with what was being dished out to him through her mouth.

It still stung a bit when I thought that my dad hadn't seen many of my baseball games or that I wasn't in many of the home movies. But, when I think about it, I did get this.

It was a very enlightening night.

###Author's present day reflections: 1) Volumes of information can be transmitted with out the utterance of a syllable, 2) There is an art of knowing when to speak, and more-so when not to.

Chapter 16
"The Day After Thanksgiving"
age 15 3/4

The word "normal" is so abusive. It minimizes those of us who strive to maximize each juicy ounce of the day.

Is it "normal" to pick a 4th Thursday in November and require everyone present to gorge themselves with turkey, dressing, potatoes, sweet potatoes, sweet peas, green beans, carrots and two casseroles whose names I cannot pronounce, but they are sweet and delicious. And after the feast comes the desserts; pecan pie, chess pie, caramel cake, chocolate cake, and one can hear someone outside cranking a home made ice cream churn.

Yesterday, I said: "Woe is me!" I have just engorged myself to the point where I don't think I can walk, and I certainly can't sit. I am in misery. I'm sure to have a fresh patch of zits to emerge on my face when I awaken in the morning if I awaken at all. This may be too much for my heart. I feel it pounding.

My plate was so full of this bounty I had to be steady to balance so not to lose or disrupt any gravy from either the turkey or the potatoes.

A little while after the feast, I hear grown men moaning over what they had just consumed. The younger people (younger than I) had the audacity to bring up the fact that someone wanted to go outside and throw a football. The only thing I wanted to throw was UP! I had a great desire NOT to throw a football.

As the grown men continued to moan, the women assumed their duty of cleaning up after all this mess which was made, the dirty dishes, the dirty pots and pans, and the left over food. It seemed a little odd that those who prepared it in the first place were expected to clean it also. I will have to ponder upon that.

My sister, knowing my pain, asks me, "Shall I call Alvin?" That was a family joke. When one of us would have a really bad cold, the flu, measles, or whatever malady, the question was always: "Shall we call Alvin?" Alvin Carter owned and operated the only black funeral home in town. He is an undertaker. He is a good friend of mine and my family. He also uses the same vehicle for both an ambulance and a hearse. It just depends upon the day and the occasion.

After the men moved away from the table, they started talking about either one of two things, a) the predicted outcome of the Ole Miss vs. Mississippi State football game, which is being played right now and we are listening to the golden voice of Jack Crystal give the play by play action., or b) their upcoming deer hunt, whose season begins the day after Thanksgiving.

I actually had more interest in learning how to hunt deer than I did the football game. My dad did not like to deer hunt, so it did not come naturally for me. But most of my cousins suffered from "deer fever", which is described as whenever a deer is in sight, in or out of hunting season, the trigger finger starts to shake. I look upon that as some kind of weird palsy.

But do I actually think someone would invite me to stay and hunt with them? Absolutely not. I am an artistic child. I sing. And I play a musical instrument. Therefore, I am not worthy of such. But that's not my point, because even if they HAD asked me to accompany them, I could not possible go. I was "taken."

It had become tradition, "normal" for me, on the day after Thanksgiving, that my Mama owned by soul, my body, and all my strength. And it was I who really needed all three to endure.

For "normal" for me on today, the day after, was for me to arise early, 6am, and prepare to accompany her on a day long trip to and from Memphis, Tennessee and shop the hours which were not taken up in travel, which is 150 miles each way. No, I am an accomplice. The goal: go to Goldsmith's, her favorite department store, and shop until she found exactly what she wanted, which was a total unknown, even to God himself, until she find it. And she WILL find it. And, yes, she did have an account there, and a few of the sales associates smile at us as if they vaguely remember us from one year ago, and the year before, and the year before that.

My mother has a "thing" for dishes, and even a bigger "thing" for shoes. No one knows why. It must go way back, maybe to prehistoric women making shoes from hides and making clay pots. Well, here we are again, repeating the pattern.

It seems really strange. It seems as though she intuitively knows how many shoe boxes and how many dish boxes can fit into our car. I think that goes way back as well. And here I am, clueless.

Undoubtedly, we would make the trek back to West Point with new sets of china, and new boxes of shoes. Last year, I specifically remember one set she purchased, which we still use. They were, and still are, colored with a yellow base and have white and blue flowers on them. They were pretty, but, hey, that stuff really doesn't float my boat. But I know much better than to utter a sound. This was not my place. This was not my role this day. I am to do what I am told, and be the companion for the day.

As I load all the newly acquired treasures into our car, I get into the passenger seat. I do not yet have my license. My permit comes next year, but I do know how to drive. She gets into the driver's seat, and we start to pull away headed back toward Interstate 55 South. She turns on the radio, and we listen to a local station playing a favorite song of hers, Andy Williams singing "Moon River". Then she asks me THE question, "Would you like to drive?" I immediately say "Yes Mam." Then she tells me to be especially careful and go kinda slow.

Lamar Avenue in Memphis is a big street-literally. In some areas, it has 3 lanes for each side! We have to be careful. We have begun our trip home, thank God, and Mama looks at the gas gauge, and says we best stop and fill up. We are already in the far right lane anticipating an exit to our right onto I-55 South toward Oxford. I spot a Shell station in up the street and tell Mama. She nods her head in approval, and we turn into the station lot. I hop out and begin the pump. I listen to the bell ring as every gallon is poured into the tank. Eight gallons, then nine. I have a little quirk about me. I like round numbers. I can't explain it. So, rather than fill it up completely, I stop it at exactly 10 gallons. Mama had the window down and I asked where the gauge was. She said full, so I was satisfied I got close enough. Mama handed me a five dollar bill, and I walked into the store and paid $4.20 for the gas, and I had .80 cents in my hand. Since we had gotten a sandwich at Goldsmith's, I was not particularly hungry. But I did decide to get a Coka-Cola. I said Coka-cola, but that's really a generic term for a soft drink. I actually chose a Bubble-UP. Those are my favorite. The Bubble-UP costs me 10 cents, and now I have 70 cents in my pocket. Mama says to keep the change. I learned a long time ago when the change is less than five dollars, I usually am told to keep it. This has become a really efficient method of me having some "running around money."

It was a good thing to see most everybody yesterday, Thanksgiving. It was especially good to remember my Mother's dad, Granddaddy. He was missed. That eye in the glass looking right back at me is still there. Why on Earth did Grand Mama want to keep THAT?

I'm still not over that "gorilla hug" I received from Aunt Gracie yesterday. She's really not my aunt, but everybody calls her that, so I do too. She is a very large woman. She is as big as a small house, and has a heart that wants to share love with everyone, everywhere. When she smiled at me when she first saw me, I knew pain was eminent.

She grabbed me and hugged on me like a Sumo wrestler. I am just so thankful she found me before the meal, and not after.

It's Friday night, and I am missing Gunsmoke, of my favorites on TV. But the trade off is good.

I take the driver's seat from the gas station. It is heavenly. Here I am cruising a Buick Electra 225 down I-55. It is so cool. On down the road, I see a sign for Oxford, but that's not for me. I continue onward until I see the sign for the Natchez Trace. That's my exit.

From that point onward, it is a dreamy Mississippi night. I am on a 2 lane highway and not much traffic at all.

There is a full moon, and I can see the moon shadow of the car, and I can actually see myself in the shadow. The pine trees on both sides of me seem to cut a path just for me. I feel like I could open the window and give a gentle blow and move a chosen star to any location I wanted across the sky.

As we get closer to home, we see Walker's Lake, the place I mostly fish, and the water is shimmering brightly as we pass by it on my right. This is heavy deer hunting country, and I don't have much traffic, so I guess the hunters have turned in for the night. But not me, I am at the helm of a mighty ship sailing to a well-known port of safe harbor.

It's just me in this Wonderland. My head lamps shining ahead spot something other than the road. As I get closer, I see an opossum family crossing the road. I gently slow down so they can cross in safety. Here goes mama and six babies in tow. Opossums are strange creatures, often found hanging by their tails on tree limbs. I am then reminded of my dad's story of his dad finding an opossum in the woods and capturing it, to bring it home. Then for a week, he would feed it only corn to clean him out, and then it would be Sunday dinner. And, yes, my dad does say they taste just like chicken. Then he would laugh and continually remind me there are more chickens roaming the earth than there are humans.

We now are pulling into the driveway at home. My back is needed to unload all the newly acquired treasures for my mom.

This day started out a little rough, but has a pure magical ending.

####Author's present day comment: 1) When I am stuck, make the best of it,

do I give it the power over me, or can I flow with it, 2)Sometimes, without warning, dreams can plop down into my lap....enjoy, 3) It's all about how I finish, not how I begin.

Chapter 17
When Huntin Ain't Just a 'Huntin
Fall. Age 17, 1971

Paul, my huntin' buddy and best friend, told me last Saturday that next Saturday, there would be a huge dove shoot, at a place I had never been. Naturally, he invited me to go along. He mentioned his Daddy, Mr. Tony, arranged this hunt. Now, I know something big is in the brew. Paul tells me dozens of his uncles cousins, etc. are coming from Birmingham. Remember, Paul is very Italian and comes from a gigantic family.

It's Friday, and I am preparing for this hunt tomorrow. Since there will be so many people, I know I will be shooting birds that fly closer to me, so I will use my smaller shotgun, a Franchi 20 gauge. That's really my favorite gun. It's an Italian shotgun weighing only 4 lbs. My Daddy gave that to me when I was 12. It is a collectors item, highly engraved, with a shiny stock and a poly-choke, which enables me to control the pattern of the pellets coming out from small to large. I wonder if any of Paul's cousins in Italy made my gun. I wouldn't doubt it. I buy 4 boxes of shells today, not knowing what to expect. One can never have too many shells. I have learned that lesson.

Paul does tell me we are going to a place close north of here near Tupelo, where we have picked up dozens of arrow heads, and a few shell casings left from the Civil War.

Earlier today, in Mississippi History Class, we did something a little out of the norm. We went on a field trip. The teacher arranged for a school bus to take us to the local library in West Point. It's called The Carnegie Library. Andrew Carnegie helped so many small Southern towns get libraries after the War. I have been to that library many times, but today I experienced the basement. It was a Confederate Museum. It smelled really musty when we walked in. It had a cement floor, not carpet. We saw genuine items from that War that killed more Americans than any other other War in our history, including WWII. We saw how they made their bullets, and how they melted the lead. We saw sabers, rifles, and pistols, all revolvers. Also, we saw forks, plates, and kitchen items. We also saw uniforms, and some of them had holes in them where the bullets entered.

I am excited about this trip, for a lot of reasons.

It's Friday night before the hunt. Paul is over at my house and we are cleaning our guns. My Daddy, early on in my huntin' lessons, taught me that an empty gun was almost as dangerous as a loaded one. I remember him telling me that most people don't take the time to make absolutely sure the gun is empty before cleaning it. He says, "Therefore, I think it's best to treat an empty gun as if it's loaded." I have not forgotten that.

While he was telling me that a few years ago, I know what was going through his mind as he was instructing me. When I was about 10, he had a close friend, accidentally put a .22 caliber bullet through his head, killing him, as he was cleaning that small pistol. Their families and ours were close. They have 3 boys distributed closely in age to our own family. It shocked the entire town and it really hurt my Daddy. That's why he's drilled that kind of gun safety since he first took me out shooting years ago. I can't imagine how that so preventable accident affected that family then, now, and forever.

About 6, Daddy comes home, and comes in to see us. He observes closely and compliments they way we are handling our guns. He looks at our work, calls it "good," and gives us both a nod of approval. Then he leaves to see all the girls in the house.

A little later, Paul and I go to the movie theater in West Point. It's called "The Ritz." I have heard there's a Ritz in New York City. I'm sure it's basically the same thing, but probably the same size. After all, ain't a movie theater just a movie theater? We see a movie called "The Great Escape". It's staged in WWII. Boy, there's a bunch of fighting! I love Steve McQueen, and I got chill bumps when he jumped that German fence on a motorcycle. I couldn't possibly make a jump like that on my own motorcycle. I loved the movie, but I do know that it was based on reality. And that reality was horrifying.

Later in the evening, Paul tells me the hunt tomorrow is near Corinth, Mississippi. That's Sucatanchi Indian country. I get excited. I like that area of the state. There's a lot of history around there, from from the Indians and also the "War Between the States."

That's a "behind the scenes" nickname for what others call the Civil War. The reason for that is that most people think that the was was exclusively about slavery. I hate slavery in any context, and the North was right to win it. The North sure thought its was all about slavery, and that was reason enough, but the South maintained the war was about a.) slavery, and b.) state's rights. The reason for that is that the North had all the industry. All the South had was labor and was totally agriculturally based.

This area was heavy in Indians, because of the agriculture. There were Chickasaw, Choctaw, Oktibeeha, They grew maize, what we know as corn, and trading with the northern Indians via the nearby Natchez Trace. How they buried their dead has always been fascinating to me. They buried their dead in mounds, and many of them are still very visible. That's where we would find the most arrow heads. And they are all different. Each tribe had a different way making an arrow head. And we have gotten to know each one.

The Battle at Corinth was an accident waiting to happen. There were and still are two main railroads that converge and intersect there. The Mobile and Ohio, and The Memphis and Markton railroads were the ones. The tracks showing the convergence are a tourist attraction now. There was also a huge battle in nearby Iuka County called the Battle of Iuka. Both battles were fought in the fall of 1862. Between those 2 battles, casualties and losses were in excess of 7,000.

The only issues I have ever had with the North were these: a.) The North knew the ENTIRE economy of the South was driven by agriculture. The decimation of the entire economy was not necessary nor was it productive, and, b.) The eradication of slavery was absolutely necessary, but the burning of all the farm implements, all the cattle, horses, and homes was not necessary nor productive. History books that show how long it took for the South to recover undoubtedly proves my point.

We leave about 6 am on this beautiful, crisp Saturday headed for Corinth. It's about 1 ½ hour drive. We go in his Plymouth Duster, the same one we strap that big metal boat onto in the Summer for fishing. We could go in my car, the Model A Ford, it would just take longer. But it is worthy. I keep it in great condition. We go North on U.S. 45 N. We pass out of our county into Chickasaw County. The county seat there is Okalona. We are very close to Choctaw Co. We then cross into Lee County, named for Robert E. Lee. The county seat there is Tupelo. That's where Elvis Presley was born. I have seen his birthplace. It's a house not much bigger than my bedroom at West Point.

It is very tiny.

We pass through Corinth, and make a left turn on a dirt road. I have the directions Paul gave me earlier.

We get to the place, and lots of people have already arrived. There are about 20 shooters. And I see something that I have never seen before. There are about 12 kids about 10 or 11 years old there. They are not shooters. They are what Paul calls, "Bird Boys". I have been on hunts using "Bird Dogs", but not this. Wow! There is a distinct voice in charge. He welcomes us and asks that all shooters gather. He then puts out the words for the hunters. The limit of birds today is 20 birds per gun. And every shooter has been preassigned a spot surrounding the field. We are instructed that every 15 minutes, there will be a 10 minute recess where the boys can go get the fallen birds. Guns will be laid on the ground and one hand held high, for safety. Dove can come from anywhere, anytime, from high, or from low. And when they land, they liftoff like a missile. All of us are cautioned to be aware of fellow shooters. All of us are instructed to announce themselves to show their whereabouts. I am instantly reminded of how Granddaddy lost an eye to this type of shooting. I have my sun glasses on.

Paul is positioned immediately to my right. That makes it more fun because we can whisper back and forth. Immediately to my left is Paul's Uncle Benny. I wonder what he's going to do, given his condition. He has no arms or legs, just nubs. This seems odd. As Paul and I open our shell boxes, I notice Uncle Benny has only one box. And then, I see him, with nubs, put 5 shells back into his box, leaving him only 20 shells. This is getting more interesting by the minute. I look over at Paul, and he just smiles. He obviously knows something I don't.

As the morning shoot begins, we hear shooting from the other side, but see no birds coming our direction.

After sitting still for about 20 minutes, the dove really start pouring in, from what seems every direction. Most everybody gets a shot every 3 or 4 minutes.

I am absolutely amazed at how Uncle Benny picks up his shotgun, props it against his nub shoulder, and fires away.

We are now having some kind of fun! Paul and I both already have 4 birds, and both of us have shot 8 times. Uncle Benny has shot 4 birds, with 4 shots. NOW, Paul begins to laugh. He now tells me Uncle Benny is really, really good.

By 11am, I have 9 birds, Paul has 8, and Uncle Benny has 11 birds, and has shot 11 times. Paul and I both have almost used one full box of 25 shells.

I am a little stunned. I don't know what to think or feel. This highly handicapped person is a perfect shooter! How does he do this? Again, I ask, how could this be? And, who REALLY IS the handicapped one here?

By noon, Uncle Benny has 20 birds and has shot 20 times, and has 5 shells left. He says to us, "I'm going in, boys, I don't like the heat in the afternoon."

My mouth needs help from dropping to the ground, from deep humiliation. I gotta laugh. Paul and I both have less than half the limit, and have half of the day left, and a severely handicapped person has just left with his limit.

There is a begging question that again haunts me, "Who's the real handicapped person here?"

We take a lunch break to catch our breath, and I try to get over MY humiliation! Paul knew it was coming——but that rascal just didn't tell me a word.

By around 4, both Paul and I have two things; 20 birds each and REALLY sore shoulders.

After we clean the birds, we walk over to thank the hosts for having us. It has been one fine day. We stop in Okalona to get some cool drinks.

During one of the breaks in conversation, I think back of a man I heard just a few years ago, Dr. Chester Swor. I remember him being a severe victim of a cruel disease, Polio.

Then, a 2 by 4 to my head could not have been more powerful than the thought of Dr. Swor saying many times during his talk, "It's not so much with what you have, but what's important is what you DO with what you do have."

This day has been quite the surprise. I learned a lot today.......mostly about myself.

####Author's present day comment: 1) Knowing history of all types is very valuable, 2) in war, there are no winners, 3)People who appear handicapped often surprise me, 4) It's a good thing for me to be joyful for the things I do have, and not to be bitter about things I don't, 5)Try to learn something about myself each day.

Chapter 18
How Can This Be?"
Age 17

It's Saturday morning, and everybody is moving a little slower this morning.

Most of the time, there is something to laugh about at my house. Either it's a funny story from my precious Willie Mae about something going on at her house or neighborhood. Just recently, Willie Mae was telling us about her next door neighbor, a lady named Miss Suzie. She lives alone on the corner in a small house. I drive by it every time I pick up Willie Mae and bring her home. Apparently, Willie Mae and Miss Suzie were talking in one of their homes sometime last week. They were talking about the United States putting a man on the moon. Willie Mae was expressing her amazement of such a feat. Miss Suzie quickly quipped, "That didn't happen. That's not possible. How could that possibly be?" Willie Mae knew Miss Suzie has a TV which in on all the time. But that made absolutely no difference in her perspective. She simply refuses to believe that a man could be traveling away from Earth in a space ship and land on the moon, walk around for a bit, stuck a U.S. Flag on it, and safely return to Earth. All the evidence pointing to the authenticity of the event has no bearing whatsoever. What

I find so interesting about Willie Mae's story is that at certain times, in certain situations, people simply believe what they want to believe, regardless of factual evidence. In addition, people feel challenged and sometimes defensive when a truth is brought forth which threatens their position.

I THINK way too much. Why can't I just be a normal teenager?

I just laugh at Willie Mae's story and go about my day, which has just beginning.

The kitchen has been the center of activity with Mama and Willie Mae telling stories. Now I hear Daddy and Maggie in the playroom laughing. It's time to investigate since I have just finished my grits and biscuits.

There, I find Maggie and Daddy enjoying a roaring fire in the fireplace. I guess Maggie built it earlier. Maggie is telling Daddy a story. She is here for the weekend since her husband Mark is in the Army Reserves and is committed to one weekend a month. They live in a small town in Alabama. Sister Ruth is married and presently has two children.....but before the ink is dry here, she might drop another one.

I have a hard time picturing myself as their "Uncle Ray" when I am 17. Like normal, while telling the story, Maggie is flailing her arms and constantly moving while telling the story. I come in at the tail end of the story and don't inquire. Maggie has a "spark" to her. Daddy has always liked that. He laughs more with her than with anybody else in the family, I think. Not to be misunderstood, Daddy loves all of us dearly. But all three of us are very different. Ruth got the brains of the offspring, Maggie got the comedy and spunk, and me.....still being defined. Daddy calls Maggie "Miss Sunshine" and says when she comes into the room, all the lights in the room light up. I agree. I think Maggie got that from Mama, but in double portion.

Daddy is reclined on the couch with his left leg elevated. Five months ago, he was bitten by a Brown Recluse Spider. Those are nasty spiders. They are sometimes lethal. Strange things happen to my dad. We think this spider came in with some newly installed carpet in their bedroom. He felt a small sting on the back of his ankle, saw it, killed it. It bit him on the Achilles's Tendon. That's the big tendon on the back of the foot. A few days after the bite, the skin and tissue around that area just sloughed off, leaving a gaping hole and a badly damaged tendon.

He has not been able to work, putting an extra burden on Uncle Harvey, his partner. We have been putting one inch squares of gold leafs to facilitate healing. It's almost healed, but not quite. Undoubtedly, this will leave him with a distinct limp.

It's a bit ironic to me that his dad, also a country Doctor in Mississippi, walked with a limp. Earlier in his life, while working as a Cowboy, he was thrown from a horse and received a broken leg. The leg was not "set" properly, producing the limp. I never knew him, unfortunately. He died before I came along. But I hear remarkable stories about this man.

Daddy explains to me Maggie has been telling him of the oddities that go on in Mama's Choir. Both Maggie and I sing in her choir, but are temporary, not knowing the inside stories. Daddy laughs and tells me about a spinster in the choir named Billie Fran Manaker. All I know about her is that she wears black Army Boots. Maybe that's the reason nobody has ever married her. Anyway, Daddy reports that Billie Fran sits in the choir loft, and then after every service, complains to Mama about all the men in the congregation making "eyes" at her in the service. That's laughable. <u>How could this possibly be?</u>

And then Maggie chimes in and tells me the time a bass named Dozo Digant was scheduled to sing a duet with my mother, who has a beautiful alto voice. On the Sunday to sing, he showed up and told her he had stage fright. She thought nothing of it. When it was time to sing, only my mother rose. She turned to him and gave him a death stare, which I know well. Then my mother turns toward the congregation and signals the organist to start. She sang only the alto line from this alto-bass duet from Bach. She did it beautifully and very few people outside the choir know the mistake. We did not joke her about that for months, but now it's OK. Dozo still sings in the choir, but has not been asked to so any specials.

And then, Maggie gets tears while telling me. It's a well known fact that the church organist, a brilliant pianist, who has cut an album, sometimes has a drinking problem. He is an extremely gifted musician. Maggie tells me one Sunday last year, he came to church a little tipsy, and it's an 11 am service. He played the prelude, the intro to worship, the hymns, and the anthem without flaw. But when it came to playing the offertory, he did something only a trained musician's ear could discern. He played a complicated, absolutely captivating piece. It was highly, highly disguised. Actually, the tune he as playing was "Take Me Out to the Ball Game." But there were only 2 people who noticed it, and one of those was my mother. Another death stare. She laughs later and asks "How could this possibly be?"

Not it's after lunch and we all are just hanging around. It's really getting colder. Thanksgiving is just a few short weeks away. I have just returned from taking Willie Mae to her home. Before I sit down, someone knocks on the side door, the one we normally use, which is by the kitchen. I open it and I see an unfamiliar face. He sticks out his hand and introduces himself as Jimmy Joe. I shake his hand and immediately notice this man desperately needs to see a really good dentist. He asks me, "Is Dr. R.B here?" I say, "Yes, but he's not taking patients right now". He says, "I'm not sick, I just want to pay him". I say, "OK" and go to tell Daddy. Daddy limps to the door and greets his friend Jimmy Joe. Daddy invites him in, but in his humility, he refuses. He asks if Daddy could just walk a few paces. Daddy graciously does so.

In the driveway, Daddy and I see Jimmy Joe's pick-up truck and a livestock trailer attached. Jimmy Joe explains he has no money to pay Daddy for saving his daughter from pneumonia, but he does say, "I brought you my prized pig. He weighs over 600 pounds." Daddy graciously thanks him for the payment. Jimmy Joe explains this pig is very tame and will make a wonderful Thanksgiving meal. My jaw drops to my foot.

Daddy says to me, "Boy, go get a rope." I turn to go get the rope and ask myself two things; 1. Why did they bother to give me a name?, and 2. How could this possibly be?

I return with a rope and give it to Jimmy Joe. He climbs into the trailer, ties the rope around his neck, and then gives me OUR NEW 600 POUND PIG! Jimmy Joe again thanks Daddy for his care for his daughter and then leaves. It's me, Daddy, and our brand new pig. I say, "Daddy, do you realize we live in town"? He says he's already figured this one out. He says, "Go tie the pig to the basketball pole, and we'll get someone to come get him or her Monday since this is the week-end". I say, "How could this be? How could you do that?" He responds in his classic softness, "I could not possibly embarrass this man in any way." Enough said. My Daddy is elevated on my short list of heroes.

He says he'll tell Mama. I can't miss what's coming so I lead the pig quickly. He's pretty easy to lead, grunting all the way. Apparently, he's not used to moving very fast. It just doesn't make sense to me that this animal (a pig) is higher on the intelligence scale than my dog, Fella. How could this be? How could this be possible? I tie him to the basketball pole and rush inside to hear. Daddy explains to Mama and she starts laughing and says "Well, it IS cold enough to kill hogs". Maggie is mortified and can't contain herself laughing so hard. I tie up Fella at the patio next to the house and try to keep him relatively quiet. I am not quite sure if Fella has ever had an encounter with a pig, and I really don't want to go there.

That evening, the four of us have a lite supper. One Sunday nites, we usually get carry-out from a local BBQ place called "The Little Pig." A little bit of irony here, don't cha think? I drive out to the place and get the sandwiches. They smell great. It's pulled pork, with a lite vinegar BBQ sauce and then they top it with cole slaw. The fries are greasy, but they are seasoned and really good. Daddy asks the blessing and even gives thanks for our new 600 pound pig. Mama looks out the window seeing the pig and then takes a bite of her sandwich. The atmosphere around this table, around this situation, is so far beyond reality it's just too hard to soak it all in.

About 10:30 that night, I notice I have not seen Daddy in a while. I walk back into their bedroom without notice and then proceed to their bathroom, again without notice. I look in the bathroom and see my Daddy with his head tilted high and his mouth attached to a big bottle of Vodka.

I turn and walk away without being noticed. I think "How could this be, how could this be possible?"

####Author's present day comment: 1)Situations beyond belief can be really funny, 2)"Take me out to the ballgame" takes on a completely new meaning,

3)When given in real humility, a payment of a debt which weighs over 600 pounds is acceptable, 4) Irony.....a God given perception, 5) How can my hero disappoint me so much?

Chapter 19
Age 17
Controlled chaos

After discovering my Daddy with an upside down bottle of Vodka, I go into my bedroom, sit down on my bed, and turn of the TV for distraction. My mind is raising with many conflicting thoughts. What is the problem here? Is is drugs? Is it alclhol? Does mama know? Does anybody else know but me? How serious is this? Has it been going on for long? If so, for how long? Was it <u>really</u> Vodka in that bottle?

There has to be a logical, reasonable explanation to this.

It's about 10:45 PM. Maggie is out with some friends and might spend the night out. I think about talking with Mama, but it's late and she has to get to church early tomorrow morning. I think it's better if I keep this to myself for a little while. I don't want to use start anything unnecessarily.

Mama Walks by my room, sees me and comes over to kiss me good night. It takes me about ½ second to say to myself, "I don't want her to go in there and get the shock of her life". I say to her, "I'm sleepy, so I'll walk with you and say goodnight to Daddy." We both walk into their bedroom and see him now sitting on his side of the bed. He turns to us, smiles, and asked me what I'm watching on television.

I respond, "Nothing really, just 'Saturday Night Live'." He gets up, walks and acts normally, walks around the bed, kisses Mama good night and says, "Come on, boy, I'll watch a few minutes with you". I say to myself, "This should be very interesting." I go to my room, stretch out on my bed and he comes in and sits in a nearby chair. I am straining to be of part of a normal conversation. I see no evidence of drinking in his speech, his eyes are clear, his walk is normal, with consideration for the limp he has because of the spider bite.

I'm totally confused!

After about 20 minutes of talking, I tell him I'm tired and am ready to go to sleep. He says OK, gets up, and leans over to kiss me. I notice nothing unusual and smell nothing. He then says he's going into the kitchen to make a "Dagwood" sandwich (That means huge). This is getting more confusing by the moment. Was I seeing things? This all seems so sureel. I turn off the television set, look at the blank ceiling for a while, just thinking, and finally drift off to sleep.

I woke up this Sunday morning with the wonderful aroma of momma frying sausage. This is not really normal for her on a Sunday morning, but evidently she got a earlier and get more done than usual. She just started to serve us sausage after labor day. This is another one of her funny little quirks. She is a one who likes variety. For six months of the year, we eat bacon in the morning. For of the other six months, we eat sausage. Go figure. It doesn't make any sense to me, either. On the other one of her little quirks is that when we go out to a new restaurant, and after the food is served, she looks around everybody's plate. If she sees anything interesting on someone else's plate, she hands them her fork and says, "Let me have just a bite of that." While I'm on the subject of her quirks, I have never heard this woman sneeze just one time. If she sneezes at all, she always sneezes seven times. It's a common family funny. Nobody has ever been able to figure that one out.

Anyway, I better get up and get my shower before Maggie or I will have no hot water. I walk into the kitchen and say good morning and tell her I'm going to take a shower before breakfast. On the way to my room, I see Daddy coming for breakfast. He seems perfectly fine. Wow! Maggie did home last night, and since it's my duty to take her back to college in Columbus later today, I'll speak with her then. My friend Paul usually accompanies me when I take her back to college, but today I call him after church and tell him I had to talk with Maggie about some Christmas gifts for Mama and Daddy. So I will lie, a little.

Mama leaves the kitchen after doing server role minor miracles of preparation. She walks over to the perolator to refill her coffee cup. I think again of Daddy's funny remark of Jesus Christ using Mama's coffee to wake the dead because it's so strong. It seems to pour into her cup like molasses.

Since Maggie and I will use my car to go to church, I will not be attending Sunday school, so we leave a little later and sing with with Mama's choir.

I shake my head when I think of "my car." When I turned 15 and got my driver's license, my Daddy presents me with a car....... of sorts. It's a 1929 Model A Ford. Baby blue. When I first received it, I did not know what to say. It was <u>not</u> what I had in mind. In reality, I kinda resented it for awhile because the other kids my age have normal cars. But not me. And I did thank him...a few moments later. But did I mean it? Debateable.

Then the shock came. Wherever I went, this car was a "girl magnet." Go figure. That's just one more way I don't understand girls..... At all.

So it's a normal Sunday. Maggie and I are in the choir which Mama directs. The organist seems quite sober this morning. What a blessing. Maggie sings soprano and I am a tenor. During the anthem, Mama is smiling at us while directing, then she gets back on the task at hand. But Maggie and I know how pleased she is that we sing with her when we can. It's now 11:20 AM and I see Brother Dinas get up to begin his sermon.

I think of a good thought. A few weeks ago Maggie and I were singing with the choir more regularly. I never will forget what trick was played on my Mama. We we preparing to sing an anthem called "Deep Water." It has a strong bass and tenor piece. All the altos and all the sopranos got together and decided to have some fun. This is a goofy group. The women decided to sing "Row, row, row, your boat, gently down the stream" in perfect sync and harmony as the men when my Mama signaled and brought in only the men. It was absolutely hilarious!

Everybody was having a ball! Mama got red faced laughing so hard. I wish I could see her do that now.

As Brother Dinas starts to speak, I see the double doors on the left side of the back of the sanctuary open up. It's my Daddy with a cane backed chair in his hand. As the sermon begin, Daddy takes his normal position. I am really freaked out about what's going on inside of me. I can't wait to talk to Maggie later.

At Sunday Dinner, Maggie tells me she wants to be at the college around five, so that means I have to leave about 4:15 or 4:20, because we are taking my car. It doesn't go quite as fast as everybody else. It's normally a 20 minute drive, and everybody passes me, and I as no one. Maybe that's the reason Daddy bought that thing for me, to keep me from going fast. If that's it, " mission accomplished."

After Dinner, Maggie and I help clean the dishes and put them away. Mama is understandably tired and wants to take a nap. So does Maggie after a long night. Daddy announces the same desire.

I am not one to "tippy toe" to a roundhouse. Nor am I a person who loves to take a nap. Never have been. So, I change clothes, get my rifle, and call my dog, Fella. We get in the car and go out into the county to a place where Paul and I usually target practice. But today I think I need to be by myself. I need to sort some things out. I have to think some things through. I take some paper plates with me and a big black magic marker, so I can make some targets with circles drawn. I also take some clothes pins from the laundry room so I can attach the targets to a post or a fence.

While shooting, I notice my holes in my targets are just a little left of center, not where I want them. I use my pocket knife, which has a small screwdriver in it, to make a few minor adjustments in the right-left direction. I don't mess with the elevation. I have that perfectly adjusted. It takes me a few moments to do this. I look up, and don't see my dog, Fella. I put my two little fingers in my mouth and given out a loud whistle for him. In about 30 seconds, he appears in sight and is now running forward me. Evidently, there was something interesting to him about 75 yards away.

I take a few shots at 25 yards, then take a few more at 50 yards. The shots are right in the small area of the target. My adjustments are "right on the money". I usually don't take any shots past 50 yards because if I do, I start to lose accuracy because of gravity and loss of velocity. Now, I know for <u>sure</u> Paul is no match for me. He regularly shoots better than me with a pistol, but rifelry belongs to <u>me</u>.

It's now 3:45 in the afternoon, so I decided to head back to the house and get ready to take Maggie back. On the way home, I stop and get $5.00 worth of gas to last me the next week. While getting the gas, I spill a little gasoline on my hands, so I go into the bathroom inside the gas station so I won't have to listen to Maggie complaining.

I am a little anxious, looking at my watch. I want to get this talk done.

After putting her things in my car, we leave at 4:15. Immediately out of the driveway, she asked, "This thing got a heater?" I say nothing and turn the heater on. It's a good thing that I've been driving around and the engine is now warm enough to put out some hot air in the heater. Good thing she didn't request air conditioning. I can't provide that. They didn't have air conditioning to put in this car in 1929. Summers are tough.

I turn onto Mississippi highway 50 east headed for Columbus, where the college is.

We pass Uncle Harvey's place on the left about a mile out of town. I opened up the can of worms that I dreaded. I said, "I've got to talk with you about something serious."

She says what she normally says, "Go for it, Boy, I'm all ears." She's always been there when I needed her. And vice versa. Other times we fight like cats and dogs.

I am also close with Ruth, my older sister. It's just that she's married, far away, having lots of babies. This is not the time to bring this up with her. If it's real, I'll deal with that later.

I tell her what I think I observed last night. She just listens. When I finish, I ask her, "Am I nuts?" Her immediate response is "No, you are not nuts, and what you observed last night is new." She continues, "Daddy has a drug problem.....taking drugs so he can fall asleep and then other drugs to keep him going during the day......and he's addicted." I asked, "Why does he do this?" Her response both puzzled me and yet confirmed what I already knew. She says, " You see how hard he works, with no breaks, and "on call 24/7."" She then yells, "He just can't say NO!" She continues yelling, "But that doesn't make it right! He is continuing to hurt himself!" I asked, "Does Mama know?" "Yes, but don't try to get anywhere with her....she will just defend him.", she says.

I am feeling so sorry for her right now and at the same time, angry with her for not dealing with it up front. I asked, "Where does he get these drugs?" She immediately has the answer. She says, "He prescribes them for either himself for some one else, using his narcotics license." I ask, "How long has this been going on?" She responds, "Maybe two years."

She warns me again not to confront Mama OR Daddy. She describes Daddy as a person who can <u>appear</u> absolutely normal at will and is highly defensive if any hints are made.

She made an interesting observation. This is a Dr. Jeckle and Mr. Hyde story. She explained that when he would take drugs, they were normally for sleep. The "uppers" were designed to get over the effects of the "downers". She said, "Dr. Jeckle was wonderful doctor and man, and there is Mr. Hyde, continually hurting himself."(communicating with her fingers). She continued to express her own anger and compassion for him, but it was mostly anger. She knew he was and still is a wonderful, saintly man who had a problem.

There was a silence that seemed to last for weeks.

I then asked, "What am I supposed to do?" I continued, "I don't want him to continue this....I don't want him to continuing to hurt himself, it will kill him!" She said there would be an appropriate time very soon. She also confirmed with great emphasis that he would listen to me more than anybody else. She told me to "lay low" for right now. I can do that.

I let her out at her dorm and thanked her for listening to me. Her response, "Ray, you are no longer the child, you are the adult." Then she shut the door. And I now I am alone, in a variety of ways.

As I head for home, I don't know what to think. I don't fully grasp the gravity of what she just said to me, but somehow I knew that before she said it.

Two weeks to the day from that dreadful Sunday when I had my talk with Maggie, I had that opportunity.

While watching TV, Mama already sleeping, about 10:45 pm, I said, "I am about to become your best ally or your worst enemy. I know your routine of drugs and alcohol. It's killing you and your family, and your reputation. The State Narcotics Board will listen to me, and I am not afraid to make that call, but I don't want to. If you are defensive in any way, deny anything of what I say, you wil choose death. If you listen to me and do what I know to be right, you will choose life."

Then I said, "What is your choice?"

###Author's present day comment: 1)Question myself before I question others, 2)Learning how a person is self destructing is very painful,

3)Appearances can be very deceiving, 4)Be careful to get as much information as possible before I choose to condemn, 5) I am not defined by my circumstances.

Chapter 20
A Stitch in Time
Age 17

HIS CHOICE WAS TO TALK TO ME.

The CBS evening evening news has just ended. I watched it today, which is unusual. I am not particularly interested in world events, but I did want an update on the Winter Olympics, and that's the only reason I'm watching it this evening. There was another interesting story in the evening news which caught my attention. Some guy in India named Mahatma Gandhi is starting a hunger strike. My friend Paul walked in my house as that Mahatma Gandhi story was just beginning. I asked Paul, "Who is Mahata Gandhi?" Paul responded, "He's a Hindu." I then asked, "Him do What?" Paul laughed AT me, not WITH me. In the winter Olympics, the United States is not doing so hot in the sports that I enjoyed. I really like the bobsled. Those guys go really fast! And it's so cool how they use their weight in leaning a certain way to change direction or control speed in a curve. I certainly use leaning when I ride my motorcycle, but not to the degree that they do plus I can't control my speed that way either.

Paul leaves after the Sunday night news, he just wanted to come by and say hello. So, I am really alone on this Sunday night in January. Mama and Daddy are in Memphis, Tennessee for a few days. Daddy is seeing a Doctor there who is helping him get over his drug and alcohol dependency. This is a difficult time for my family. The secret is out. That's both good and bad news. The bad is the recognition of the problem, and how it could have ever been allowed to exist at all. In addition, his practice has suffered. Relationships have been betrayed. An enormous amount of judgment has been thrown toward him, some warranted and some not warranted. The good is that it's OVER! Thank the Lord our family is still intact. Many families have dissolved in some fashion as a result of stuff like this.

I am furious at him, on too many fronts to count. But I'd guess, mainly, is what he was doing to himself and others who have loved him so long. But I'm torn. Because I knew "the how", but only recently I became totally aware of "the why". I should've seen it coming. I should have known. I suspected, but did not confront. At the same time, I did not know what I did not know. The "why" is rooted in his inability to say "No", in addition to not having any hobbies. In addition, they really don't take many trips. No real vacations. He's just worked himself 3/4 to death and turned to drugs to cope.

Last week my life was changed. My hero came to me wanting to speak to me about this problem. Why me? I've found out since then the reason he came to me is because I was the only one who was not throwing stones at him. He said to me, "I have been living a lie, I have been living a double life." I just listened as he explained "the how". He knew all the tricks in order to keep up the habit yet keep it totally concealed. These were truly lethal drugs when used inappropriately. I'm thankful he did not accidentally kill himself.

He continues his talk with me, "I have ruined my life, my practice, and I'm so ashamed and broken." We walked outside and had

our coats on because of the cold. We were leaning up against his car, a 1965 white Mustang. I never understood why he chose to get an automatic transmission, rather than a stick shift. But, that was not for me to decide. I kept listening to this man, my hero, in tears. He could not believe what was happening. He could not believe how this could have been going on for so long. He went on for a good 45 minutes, and I just listened. I did not comment until later. He kept repeating, "I'm done, I'm finished." That statement pierced into my own heart just listening to him in that condition. He was completly broken.

After he finished, still weeping, I grabbed his shoulders and drew him close. I held him very tightly. I told him there was nothing he could ever do to make me not adore him. During that long pause, something happen. I'm still not sure what it was. I then told him to sit on the side of the car, and it was my turn to speak. He suggested we get in the car because it was so cold. I agreed. I got in the driver's seat, both literally and figuratively. He was seated in the passenger seat. I told him, "You have some choices to make, some of which I know and some only you could know. You are lucky you did not kill yourself you are also lucky you still have a family. We're all alive. We are all relatively healthy. You have got to get some professional help. This time, you cannot cure yourself." He nodded his head in agreement. I continued, "You must first take ownership of the mess you have created. You must ask forgiveness for this mess. I realize you did not intentionally do this. <u>Let what I just said to you sink really deep.</u> Nevertheless, it has happened. And you must deal with it. You must deal with it quickly. There is no quick a way to resolve this." Again, he nodded in agreement. I could not in the depths of my soul imagine the pain this man was experiencing. I had never seen him like this. It was just awful. It was misery, pure misery. Now, I'm thinking about that moonshine still. I wish those men had shot me dead. Then I wouldn't have to deal with this. But I am in this, and I'm a part of it. So there.

But somewhere deep inside that car on that cold January night, maybe sitting in the back seat, or in the small trunk, was a faint, yet present sense of hope.

After that conversation, we went inside. But I told him on the way inside he had to make peace with God, and after that it was time to go to Mama. He told me he had already done the former, and then instantly headed for their bedroom to speak........with her. It was a long night. I don't think I've ever been so tired, and pray I never will be again.

Not knowing and unwittingly, over the last week, I became the adult advisor to my hero. What a paradox. What an absolute puzzle whose pieces had been strewn across the South, and I am responsible for putting that puzzle back together intact. There is a TV show called "Mission Impossible." That show is child's play compared to what I see ahead.

Whew! I have been tired all week after all that happened. Willie Mae has been coming every day, fixing my meals, and making my bed. I detest making up my bed. I have been going to get her before school and a friend of hers has been picking her up before I usually arrive around 3:30 PM. All week, it has smelled mighty fine every time I've opened the side door. She has taken excellent care of me, and I'm so thankful for her. She is my mother's best friend, despite the oceans of differences in their cultures and their race. They are inseparable. Willie Mae will undoubtedly be a rock for Mama in the weeks ahead.

It's still Sunday night and my emotions are going more rampant than usual. I gather my thoughts as to what's going on at school tomorrow. Yes, I have an English test. That should be no problem. My car, the 1929 Model A Ford, is really hard to start on these cold mornings so I am prepared to go to school on my motorcycle, if needed. I'll just have to dress warmer for the short ride. I fade off to sleep reading one of my favorite books, *The Incredible Journey*.

It's Monday morning. I get out of bed and start my morning routine with a big bowl of cornflakes with a sliced banana on top, sprinkled with sugar. And I don't forget my big glass of chocolate milk.

I then put on my coat, go outside and try to start my Model A Ford. It doesn't even think about starting. I must change out those spark plugs soon. I go back into the house and called Willie Mae and tell her the news. She tells me she can get a ride to our house by calling one of her friends. That's good news.

Somehow, I just can't picture Willie Mae riding behind me on my motorcycle. But it's a really funny thought. Now that I think about it, it's a really funny thought.

I head for my bathroom and brush my teeth and put in my contacts. I gather my things, and then really start to bundle up. It appears I am ready. I exit my house through the back door. I keep my motorcycle underneath the eaves of the house on the back patio, to keep it dry from nasty weather. I get on the cold leather seat, which goes right through my jeans onto my bony butt. I turn the key on, and then press the starter button. The engine starts, and I roll it backwards a little, and then put it into first gear. I am now pulling off the patio onto the grass to go around the house and onto the driveway. As I get off the patio, the engine dies in this cold weather. The bike and I fall over to my right, straight into Mama's holly bush.

OK, I am on the ground, my bike partially on top of me, and my right foot really hurts. As I fall, my faithful dog Fella leaps from his resting place and comes to my aid.

This motorcycle is a Honda 350 Scrambler, and it is not as light-weight as my dirt bike I had before this one.

Both my arms are OK and free, so I pushed the bike up with my left arm and left leg. As I try to get up to stabilize the bike, I put the kick stand down and try to stand. I, I, I can't stand! My right foot is useless and now I'm in severe pain. I look down and see blood in my sock.

This is not good. I see more and more blood in my right sock. I take off my shoe and my sock is soaked in blood. I pulled down my sock and discover a slash and my ankle caused by that break pedal as the bike fell. There is enough blood flowing, so I have to act quickly. I take off my left shoe and sock and tie my right ankle with my left sock and apply pressure on the wound to stop the bleeding. I sit there for a moment to gather my wits.

OK, what do I do next? Should I "Call Alvin, my friend the undertaker?" Nope, not ready for that. I could go to the local ER. People know me there. But right now, there is too much anger in me and I am too ashamed to show my face there. My hero is in the hospital in Memphis dealing with his own problems. Here I am, trying to decide the best course of action.

OK, I have quickly arrived at a plan. I just simply have to execute the plan. All my friends are already at school, so that's not an option. Willie Mae does not have a car. 15 minutes have now passed, and the bleeding is not as bad as before. Knowing if I stand, the blood will rush to my foot and my efforts to stop the bleeding will have been in vain, so I scoot myself, on the ground, over to the back door of the playroom, the closest route to a bathroom. It's about 15 or 20 feet away.

While opening the door I see a few drops of blood on the brick patio. I'll deal with that later. I scoot myself toward the bathroom. I pull up my jeans on my right leg to my knee. I put my foot into the bathtub so I can take a detailed look at the wound and clean it thoroughly. I gently lower my bloody sock and see the wound. It's about 5 inches in length and in the middle there's a deep gash with the skin separated. This is a bigger wound than I originally thought. I cover it for a few more moments to stop this seepage of blood. While I am sitting on the edge of the bathtub, I reach across to the lavatory to grab a bar of soap. I know this soap. It's called SafeGuard. And I also know this soap is anti-bacterial, and that's exactly what I need at this moment. After a little time, the bleeding has stopped and I can go to work. With slightly warm water, I wash the wound thoroughly. The soap stings, but I know what it's doing. It's killing germs, so I continue withstanding the discomfort.

My Daddy says, " If you don't wash it for 15 minutes, it's not clean." So I time myself. After about 10 minutes, this is getting old, but I know better than to stop at this point.

Ah, 15 minutes have passed! This baby step of my mission has been accomplished.

Based upon my last eight years accompanying my Daddy in the local Emergency Room, I know this wound needs more help than what little I have done. I know it needs stitches, more than just one or two. I wish I was delivering a baby. That would be far easier. More planning is required. I have no transportation but my motorcycle. I could go to the ER, but, again I say, I am way too angry and ashamed to go there right now. I know I can also go to my dad's office. I have a set of keys for his office. Really, should I do this? My options are limited. After finishing cleaning the wound, I scoot myself back to my parent's bedroom and go to my Daddy's clothes closet. I find a right shoe. His feet are bigger than mine and that's what I want to use. I also know he wears support hose for socks, and I readily find a pair. I put the first one on over my foot and over the 4 X 4 gauze I got from Daddy's house call bag on the way through the kitchen. I then put the second support hose over the first. Now I know I'm good for travel. I put on one of Daddy's right shoes, and then scoot toward the kitchen. I look ridiculous. I mean, I really look ridiculous, and I am glad no one is around. His office keys are on my key ring so that's no problem.

Putting on my coat, I ask again, "Is this crazy?" A little voice answered in my head, "Yes, but move quickly."

I put on my gloves and then attempted to stand. I did feel a little blood, but not enough for concern. I am able to limp out to the motorcycle. I get on the bike, and push the start button. The engine starts quickly. The kick stand is still down, so I raise up my right foot and rest it on the handlebar while I allow plenty of time to warm up the engine.

I had learned that lesson well. After the engine is good and warm, with my left foot, I raise the kick plate and put it into first gear.

On a motorcycle like this, the right foot has an easy part. It only controls the back wheel brake. My right hand controls the front wheel brake. My right hand also controls the accelerator. My left hand controls the clutch required when I shift gears with my left foot.

OK, the bike is now in first gear. The bike was ready, but was I? That remains to be seen. Riding easily and slowly I move around the house and am now headed toward the driveway. There are no cars coming on this small street and town, so I keep moving and as soon as I got to the pavement, I shift into second gear. Gathering just a little speed, about 25 miles per hour, I shift to third gear in order to have a smooth, slow ride. There are two stoplights I must encounter plus cRuthsing the railroad tracks of the C and G Railroad Company. I see the first stoplight. Right now it's red, so I downshift to second gear to slow down a little bit. If my timing is good, I can go through this one as a green, not having to stop and risk losing my balance because of the lack of use I have with my right foot.

Success! I make it through the first one as a green. Now the second one is in sight…it's now a green, so at this speed I have no chance to make it through with a green light. I prepare to stop. I downshift and lean the bike to my left so to balance the bike on my left foot. All is well so far.

Now, it's green and I'm on my way again. I cross the railroad tracks with relative ease and I am almost there.

I reached the last stop sign before I reach Daddy's office, which is right across the street from the County Hospital, where I was born. My Daddy, with the assistance of my Uncle Harvey, delivered all three of his children in that hospital. It used to be called Flowers Hospital, until the county bought it from them several years ago. My Dad's office is to my right. It's a converted house into a medical office for Daddy and Uncle Harvey. In a stately fashion in the front yard, one of the biggest Magnolia trees in the State of Mississippi stands strong. I turned into the driveway, which usually houses my Daddy's 1965 Mustang. Now it houses my red motorcycle with me and a badly beaten up right foot. I hobble to the side door. I open the locked door. It's dark inside. I turn on some lights. It's a familiar sight.

At once, I see my speechless friend Fred. Fred is a fully assembled skeleton of a man. I have had lots of fun with him through the years, even taking his skull to school for Science class. Then I hobble onto the examination room. This room is complicated. It houses a lab with micRuthcopes all round, and X-ray machine, and a long stainless steel table with stirrups on one end. I don't even want to think about the purpose of those stirrups right now. All I am interested in doing is going to the table with which I am most familiar. The sutures and needles and Novocain are there seated on white sterile cloth. Novocain is used for numbing tissues. I turn on the examination light, which is very bright, and see my Daddy's plastic head band with magnifying lenses and a light. It also has a special microscope where he can see small particles in someone's eye. I have changed the batteries in that light many times for him. It remains untouched and very still for now.

Now for my own situation. I have the tray where the syringes are, with my choices of needles and thread. I choose those with which I am most familiar. I remember my Daddy calling the thick black thread "000 Cat Gut" (that's pronouced 'triple aut cat gut'). That doesn't make any sense to me, but at this point I really don't give a rat's behind. But I do hope this thread doesn't come from the innards of a cat.

After putting on a pair of surgical gloves, I pick up a syringe. Boy, do I miss my Daddy right now. I recognize now I am getting ahead of myself. I need to deaden the damaged tissue with Novocain. Now I place my hand on the syringe and attach a 2 inch needle and pick up the bottle of anesthesia, shake it, and turn it upside down so that I can insert the needle and retrieve the Novacaine. I draw back the plunger on the syringe about halfway, filling it with air. I then insert the needle into the bottle of Novacaine and push the plunger of air into the bottle so that I can retrieve the anesthesia. My syringe is now filled with about the same amount of the anesthesia as the amount of air pushed into the bottle. I have deadened many wounds for other people, but doing this for myself is a completely different story. I then start the deadening of tissue process. I insert the needle into my own flesh at the smaller end of the wound. It really hurts, as I am piercing my own torn flesh. I press down on the plunger a little and then move upward about an inch.

I then do the other side the same way. Then I move upward another inch on that side and repeat the process until I am at the other end of the wound. Tears are streaming from my face. Wiping tears and noses is the only use for sleeves. Both my long sleeves are soggy now.

By now, the first part which I deadened a few moments ago is actually without any feeling at all, which signals me to get busy. I now pick up a specially curved sewing needle with the thread attached. Then I grab a set of forceps to use for the actual sewing. I start at the beginning where there is now no pain. I then sew the first stitch, draw the skin close and tie my world famous fishing knot and cut the excess thread. That fishing knot that Daddy taught me is actually a surgical knot, tied with one hand. I am done with my first stitch!

Onward and upward! As I move upward toward the wider gashed area, I am careful to take note that the Novacaine has taken effect. Thankfully, it has. I have to use more thread over the wider areas because this is the widest part of the wound. Then as I move toward the other end, it doesn't require as much thread per stitch. I count the stitches I have put in so far. It's 13. That's not acceptable. Have you ever heard of a hotel that has the number 13 on the buttons in the elevator? Absolutely not! So, I put just one more stitch on the end just to cover all my bases. Now, it's an even 14 stitches. Keeping aware of how much anesthesia I used, I don't think I will have any problems. I hope it's deadend for days, but I don't get my hopes up. I keep looking at the sewed area to make sure it looks like

I've seen Daddy do it so many times. It does. I have seen him put the stitches closer together when on the face to minimize the scarring. But my foot is not my face, so I am not as concerned with a scar or not. Part of me wants a big scar so I can brag on it. But for now, I just want to finish up and go home. But not yet. I am so glad I can't feel anything. This would have been horrible otherwise.

After the last stitch has been sewn and the excess thread cut, now I have to assess the situation. No blood is seeping. The stitches look pretty darn good to me. Now, it's time to sprinkle some Sulphur on the top to help prevent infections. I turn the bottle upside down and tap it with a nuckle. The yellow powder substance is quickly dispensed. Now, it's time for the dressing. I grab a stack of 4 X 4 gauze pads and put 4 thick on 1/2 of the wound, and the other 4 on the other half. Now, it's completly covered. Now for the tape. I find surgical tape nearby and completely cover it.

After inspecting my and work and calling it "good", I now grab an

ACE elastic wrap. I do a familiar figure 8 with my wrapping. I then put on my sock and am almost ready to clean up my mess and go home. I still keep my foot elevated as much as possible and start putting things away. Undoubtedly, the nurses who come to work when my Daddy returns are going to get a shock, because I sure as the dickens don't know how to sterilize something for future use. But that's a battle I don't have to fight today. I have fought enough.

My mismatched shoes are now back on and I am able to limp with relative comfort. I turn off the lights, say good-bye to my friend Fred, and lock the door of the clinic. I am one tired puppy.

When I get to the house, Willie Mae is there. We greet each other and she asked if I was sick. I say no. She then sees my limp and asked about it. I say my bike fell over and bruised my ankle. I know when to shut up. My Daddy says knowing when to shut up is more valuable than knowing when to say something. It's almost dinner time and it smells good. Now, Willie Mae will only have to package one meal today for me.....Supper.

During Dinner, the anesthesia starts to wear off. That blasted thing really hurts! I take some pain medication in vain. It still hurts.

My friend Paul comes over right after school to see why I wasn't at school. When I explain my exploits of the morning, he simply comments, "So why did you stay home from school?" That was NOT a surprising response. It's difficult to impress Paul. After all, I am a year younger than him, in years only, not in rifle shooting accuracy. In that, I reign supreme.

Paul leaves to meet some friends at the Big R drive-in. I then start thinking about a plot to a theme for when Mama and Daddy get home from Memphis. I must remember the focus is on his recovery, not my ankle. They are due home in the next 2 or 3 days.

Several of my friends have dropped by and several of my parent's friends have dropped by as well. Willie Mae is there every day so I am well cared for. Everybody is surprised to see me hobbling around like Granpa Moses. My special friend, Angela, brings me some home-made chocolate chip cookies. That makes me smile inside and out. By now, my story is consistent. I simply fell off my bike and bruised my ankle.

I have eaten like a king. Today, Willie Mae defrosted some frozen peaches that Mama had put up and froze late in the summer for such a time as this. She has a special way of making fried fruit pies that send me to the moon, especially when they are served warm and then vanilla ice cream is on the top. It makes the pain of the wound much less severe. At a time like this, my Daddy would say, "If you have a splinter in your finger, hit your big toe with a hammer. You won't think about your finger for a while." I'm not quite at that point.

In the mornings, my ankle is understandably pretty stiff, as well as other areas of my body which were not so badly bruised.

Now that these stitches are in, I have no choice but to take a bath with my foot hanging out. It can't get it wet.

It must stay dry. These stitches will remain in for about 10 days. Daddy will be home by then. I can't think about that right now.

It's impossible to express the range of emotions I have experienced these past couple of weeks.

Author's present day reflections: 1) Living a lie is not living at all,

2) Speak heavy messages founded in deep love, 3) Notice the paradoxes in my life...they are everywhere, 4) It's amazing what I can do when my options are limited, 5) Having a plan is vitally important in most all situations,

6) You can do more than you think you can.

Chapter 21
Cold, Wet, Scared, and Tired
Age 17 Wintertime

Its January in Mississippi. It's mostly cold and wet. Those last two sentences mean the same thing. Some months are just plain ugly to me and this is one of them. Now, when I hunt, I am forces to prepare differently. The season commands that I put on heavier clothing, plus rain gear. When it rains while hunting, it's a specially miserable because the wind is so cold. These conditions don't seem to bother my faithful companion, Fella. He's ready to go any time. But we won't be taking him today.

I leave the house about 10:30 on this Saturday morning. I immediately go to Paul's house to join him. This time we look at the sky and we see promising skies for later in the day. We talk about what would be the most fun. We decided that we will take our rifles and head for the Tombigbee River, about 12 miles away.

We take my car and as we get closer, we see a more promising skies. The winter wheat growing in the fields is a beautiful green. And the tops are swaying back and forth, as if to wave. But we are definitely not in Kansas. I pull off of the highway onto a dirt road which is slightly muddy. We get out, park the car, and put on our high rubber boots so not to get completely muddy. We load our rifles to their capacity and take new boxes of cartridges in a pocket. We hope to be shooting a lot. As we walk toward to the river, we scare up some quail. They make a loud racket when they fly, unlike the silent dove. We also scare up 2 does, female deer. They run and almost float to as they jump a wooden fence effortlessly. They're beautiful and we know a buck is not too far away. It's that time of year.

Neither one of us are big deer hunters. They're just too beautiful. In addition, we don't have a license for such hunting nor do we have the right equipment. So, we simply enjoy the wintry scenery as we travel closer to the river, which is our destination.

Our destination is the railroad trustle. It's a really a bridge made of both wood and mental which crosses the river with train tracks. Freight trains from the C and G Railroad Company use that bridge to haul both cotton grains, cattle feed, and pulp wood from Columbus, Mississippi (far eastern Mississippi) to Greenville, Mississippi, which is on the Mississippi River on the western side of the state. "The Mighty Mississippi" is a big shipping port to New Orleans and then spills into the Gulf of Mexico and then goods can be shipped anywhere in the world.

Speaking of the "Mighty Mississipi", I can say, without question, the most miserable I have ever been was when a friend asked me to join him while duck hunting on that big, bad river. Big mistake. What kind of evironment do ducks like? Cold and wet. We got into a small boat and disguised ourselves in some bushes along the shore. It was raining, and a frigid wind was coming over that river on us, ripping right through me. I had no desire to shoot anything but myself to put me out of my misery. That river is terribly, terribly dangerous. It has multiple currents, running in all directions. If I had fallen in, my chances of survival would have been slim. The undercurrents are what kill people. They actually suck a person under and take them for a ride to who knows where. I shot 4 ducks and was quickly ready to go back to the cabin. My friend called me a "sissy". I was glad to accept that name so as to go ASAP to a nearby fire and some hot chocolate with marshmellows on top.

Meanwhile, back at the Tombigbee. Our interest is what's going on just beneath the surface of the water, around the concrete posts, holding up the bridge. There are four of these posts, holding the bridge about 40 to 50 feet above the river.

After walking into the marshes about 50 yards, we finally find our access point. It looks radically different now than when we come here in the Summer. We have to climb the metal railings to get to the tracks. We sling our rifles up over our backs and climb up about 15 feet. There, we find a upwardly slanted metal pole we can walk upon to get us closer to the tracks. We climb upwards about 15 more feet and there we swing ourselves onto the main metal railing which is on both sides of the tracks. We find we are less winded now than when we were climbing. We stand up, walk a few feet, and find ourselves at the big wooden railway ties, which hold up the tracks. They are big wooden 12" X 12" and must span 30 feet in length. These have been soaked in creasote, an oily solution which preserves them for forever.

We actually walk on the railroad ties between the iron railroad tracks. We take shorter steps than our normal stride so to walk on the ties. As we proceed now toward the river, we see the ground getting farther and farther away and then we are walking over water. We proceed toward the center of the river. It's a daunting task of hanging on and walking because of the cold wind coming down on our way. The sun is now shining, giving us some warmth. We sit down on the railroad ties closest to the middle of the river. We set up for the great adventure. Swimming around those giant concrete piers, at this time of day, we hope to see an ancient fish called a Garr. It kinda looks like a barracuda, which swims in the ocean, and is pretty much made of all teeth. This fish is uglier than that. They come to the surface to feed.

And, in response, we take a sharp aim and shoot as many as we can. Being about 50 feet above the water makes it a bit more difficult, but we are highly experienced at this. We mostly come here in the summer to shoot them, and also to shoot snakes in the water. It's a specially fun to shoot a rattlesnake swimming in the river. We instantly know when the snake is a rattler because he holds his rattler up out of the water and safe from getting wet. We can't tell the other snakes apart heart so easily. We just know they are all bad.

But today, no snakes. Just Garr. They are easy to shoot. They are big and slow and we are quick and deadly accurate. In reality, the only reason they're slower is because it's feeding time.

They are plentiful today. There are dozens of them swimming around the four concrete piers. Our rifle barrels get hot from all the shooting we are doing. We both have semi-automatic rifles. Paul's is a Winchester that his Dad gave him when he was 10 years old. And mine is a Remington, which my Daddy gave me when I was 10 years old.

We've been here about an hour, and we are just having an absolute blast! Earlier, before we came here, we stopped at the "Big R" drive-in and and got greasy hamburgers and and greasy French fries. We also had two king-sized Cokes in our jackets. Because of the temperature, the Cokes were still really cold. At the "Big R", I fell prey to buy two freshly made oatmeal cookies, and I've been thinking about those ever since I bought them. I really hope Paul doesn't want one. That would really put a wrench in my day. We chomp down on the sandwiches because we are really hungry. We have found a comfortable spot to sit down close to where we have been shooting. We are right in the middle of the river on the trustle. Life is good. The temperature has really risen and it's not near as uncomfortable as it was earlier.

As we finish our drinks, both of us have to empty our bladders. Ordinarily. This is a no brainer. But here, it's not so easy. We are 50 feet above the water standing on a train track. The wind is blowing relentlessly. We have several obstacles to overcome in spite of this ordinarily simple procedure. The direction of the wind is critical. Balance is critical. The direction of the aim is crucial. Otherwise, the opposite results would give the other partner amble teasing material for weeks upon weeks.

Success on both fronts! No embarrassments today. In addition, my bladder said a big "Thank you!"

Paul then asks me a sobering question. He asks, "Did you feel that?" I say, "Feel what?" " Vibration!," he says. I say, "I feel a train is coming!" He confirms.

Now we are in a dilemma. We know we must run immediately, but in what direction? From which direction is the train coming? The vibration which we both feel is becoming increasingly more intense, but it gives us know sense of comfort, only the opposite.

I have to think this through. This requires some logical, rational thought. We both know the train comes through West Point twice a day. Paul interrupts my process with "Hurry to up, I don't want to jump!" Now I am back on task. The train going through West Point in the morning always travels eastward, headed for Columbus. The one in the afternoon goes through West Point in a westwardly to direction, headed for Greenville, Mississippi.

"I've got it!", I yell to Paul.

We quickly gather are things and start running the opposite way, headed back toward my car, running <u>away</u> from the train instead of running toward it!

As we are running. Both of us are skipping railroad ties, stepping on every other one. We continue running taking great care to make no mistakes or tripping. We can't afford that now.

Now I hear a frightening sound. I hear the train engineer blowing his Whistle because he knows he must warn tugboats that he is approaching the river. The shrill of the whislte is getting louder and louder. Now the train is moving pretty quickly toward us. We are closing in on either being in or out of imminent danger....... in the next few seconds. We know this train usually travels about 25 to 30 miles per hour. We also know it will not slow down for us. It is us who must yield to its way.

These last couple of moments seem to take days! Now we both can see the train coming out of the forest into view, but is not yet on the bridge. We are not out of danger. We still have far to go.

We feel the train actually getting onto the bridge and as the train gets to the trustle, the intensity of the vibration is rattling, almost unnerving. If we can just maybe make it 30 to 40 feet more..... with no mistakes.

This type of vibration is very unfamiliar and is quite frightening. We really have to concentrate, above and beyond feeling and seeing a moving train coming straight at us while we are still high above the ground. There is no question that if we have to jump at this point there will be broken bones.

The only question remaining is how many and where, if we don't break our necks in the process.

Paul makes it to our access point about 3 seconds before me. We climb off of the railroad ties and onto the frame of the bridge. There, we hang on for dear life.

Less than 5 seconds later, we have to cover our ears from the noise of the train passing by, in addition to the rattling of the bridge itself. We remain there, with our hands over our ears, as the train passes by pulling about 60 or 70 full containers westward.

We are still very rattled, although we can breathe easier knowing at least the train won't kill us today. But we still have to climb the rest of the bridge railings to get to the marshy ground where we started.

Now we feel the train leaving the bridge.

After both of us are on the ground, we both grab hold of a tree and just stay still for a few moments. Paul sees a big stump and gingerly walks toward it to sit. I join him. There is complete silence, other than the noises which go with being on the banks of a river, as we gather our wits. After a while, I say to Paul, "As many times as we have done this, both in summer and winter, <u>nothing</u> like this has ever happened." His response, "Yeah, I know, but you know something? That train runs on a schedule. By now, we should have known that schedule."

I shake my head in agreement. Today, we had instantly acquired a little wisdom, and a little knowledge. We learn not to allow circumstances to get out of control.

Today's dramatic episode reminds me of something which my Daddy has said to me many times. He has seen scores of victims of train accidents, and none of them were trains. He says, "Don't race a train. You won't win." We've proven that today.

###Author's present day comments: 1) We should teach our young people that, contrary to their beliefs, they are not immortal, 2) When in danger, anticipate what <u>could</u> happen and move decisively.

Chapter 22

"Sweep the Ugly Truth Under the Rug" age 17, early in the year

My Daddy has always taught me about the things I experience in my own life. One of his "classics" is "There's no lower form of humanity than an ingrate, and there is no higher form of humanity than a heart filled with gratitude......for whatever."

He has also taught me to concentrate on "reading" people. It has absolutely nothing to do with judging people. It has everything to do with knowing what people are REALLY saying in their communication with me.

One obvious example of this is a car salesman. You KNOW going in his <u>agenda </u>is to try and sell you a car. Another is a person running for an elected position. He, and an occasional she, has an <u>agenda,</u> which is to convince you and me he is, without question, the best candidate for the position and will do more than he has already promised he will do. By the way, I don't know many, if any, people who <u>don't</u> have some sort of agenda. I think it's really cool to think about that when I am listening to friends, people on

TV. Sometimes it's more obvious than others, but it's usually there. Agendas are not bad. Even Jesus himself had an agenda, a really good one.

In my current World History class, we are studying the different Caesars. They are all different, but the one who fascinates me the most is Caesar Augustus. That's the same one who ruled over the Roman Empire when Mary and Joseph, the parents of Jesus, were forced to go from wherever they currently lived, back to the city of their birth. The outward agenda was so Caesar could get an accurate census.

But, when I read my own history book, and compare that to what I found in our World Book Encyclopedia, it telling me what that guy said on his dying bed, I get a totally different picture. On his dying bed, he said, "Young men, hear an old man to who old men harkened when he was young." He continued, "I found Rome a city of bricks and left it a city of gold." There's one more that blows my mind, "May it be my privilege to have the happiness of establishing the Commonwealth on a firm and secure basis and thus enjoy which I desire, but only if I may be called the author of the best possible government and bear with me the hope that when I die the foundations which I have laid out its future will stand firm and stable."

OK, now comes the underlying motive. The census which he wanted was for another purpose than what he said. It was for something totally different. If he wanted to know the population of the empire, he then would have a wealth of knowledge. And that knowledge would enable him to impose as much additional tax upon the people as he possibly could! But was that TOLD to anyone? Absolutely not. There would have been riots in the streets.

Although I don't remember who told me this, I still think it's a good saying; "What do you do with the dead elephant in the room? You either sweep it under the carpet OR you can invite it in for a cup of coffee. You have a choice." Choice? Not so in the South. Sweeping things under the carpet is the norm.

The term "sweep it under the carpet" didn't come into being in vain. On the contrary, it came into being for a variety of purposes.

But its main purpose had, and I suppose will always be: to hide something from the eyes of others.

That has always befuddled me. I am sure I have consciously and not consciously used that technique in communications to hide physical objects, like that Playboy magazine I told you about earlier. I definitely was consciously using it then!

And then there's other things we hide, like feelings, emotions, wants, desires, hurts, anger, resentment, depression.....the list is literally endless. It has to be. We are a complicated lot. I'm not sure when people say, "Times were simpler then," is totally not true. At this point in my short life, it seems to me the answer to that statement is; "from whose perspective?"

My perspective on things today is different than it was just 5 years ago. I wouldn't call it better or worse, just different.

At this moment, the biggest example of what I am speaking comes from my American History Class I am taking right now, not the World History. It gives examples of how our founding fathers, George Washington and all the others, chose to wear those ridiculous looking wigs at parties, gov't functions, and the like. And some of them got their wigs powdered! What rational thought went into that kind of thinking? Its origin is either way is way above or way below my thought process. You choose. But the question remains! What were they trying to "sweep under the carpet?" Somewhere deep down in that mess, truth was pounding at the door to get out.......maybe it still is.

And what bozo came up with a name for a hate organization named

"Ku Klux Klan?" Why couldn't they just call themselves "WHBP," which stands for "we hate black people." It was and still is a secret hate organization (sweep it out of sight). It's design is to strike fear into people of a different color than pure white and keep it out of sight (sweep it under the carpet). They wear white robes over their faces because they do not want their identities known....."sweep it under the carpet."

Why can't we call "sweep it under the carpet" what it really is: DECEPTION! It is clearly deception, and it's strewn thoughout history. But "deception" is such a harsh word. We must soften it.

The Civil Rights Amendment formally came into reality in 1964, 7 years ago. I remember it well. I lived it. I felt it. I experienced it.

The tradegy is that it had to be done at all.

One would have thought that the wording of our own beloved Constitution would have instantly gotten rid of all racism. Words like "all men are created equal" and "all have been endowed by our Creator with certain inalienable rights…….." But in truth, even some of our founding fathers had slaves <u>after</u> the the signing. What a farce.

It took a while for the DE-segregation to take effect. It took years, not months……and it's still in process. There were then and there are now tensions on both sides. The irony that I experienced back then was that the black people did not want to go to school with us whites any more than us wanting to go to school with them. They, very simply, and very justifiably, wanted an <u>equal</u> education with the white folks. Was there anything wrong with that? Absolutely NOT!

Then, I ask, why did the Democrats in Congress fight against it so hard (sweep it under the rug). In reality, they HAD the black vote because they gave the black people the "perception" that they were on their side and those filthy rich Republicans were evil and were "after" them. In reality, it was the minority party, the Republicans, who actually got it passed and that made the sitting President, Johnson, look good (sweep it under the rug). This looks like a replay of how Honest Abe, a Republican, got the Emancipation Proclamation passed.

That act of 1964 was wonderful. I am a young white male cheering on for the beleagered minority. Today, I understand more of their resentment of white people than ever, for a lot of reasons.

I'm no futurist by any means, but my sincere hope is that we don't repeat our tragic mistake we made with the Native American People. Because of our guilt, we gave them so much, they have ruined themselves. I better rephrase that. We did not allow them to meld themselves into our society, with taxes and responsibilities. The error was ours, not theirs. Let us not repeat that horrid societal mistake.

We now have an opportunity of a lifetime which could shape an entire race into the greatness our founders envisioned.

When I was younger, 6 or 7 years old, we had, I said had, a public swimming pool. It was huge. My Mama and my two evil sisters would take me there only on Mondays, Tuesdays, and Wednesdays. That familiar big metal sign saying "FOR WHITES ONLY" was there, too. I was allowed only in the smaller of the two pools, the baby pool, because

I had not yet learned to swim. Mama called that the "Pee Pool". I think the reason is quite obvious. I had no idea why we only went there on those certain days.

My sisters would meet all their friends "at the pool." Those were really fun times. At that's the place where those gigantic wisteria vines grew, too. The smells in the early Spring were beyond description. I have heard people say those vines covering the canopy were well over 100 years old. I know they have seen some neat stuff.

When I was 8, Mama arranged for me to take swimming lessons. That was fun. Nita Chandler was my teacher. She and my sister Ruth were and still are good friends. Lessons were held on Mondays, Tuesdays, and Wednesdays, from 11am-1pm. I was a quick learner of swimming. I guess I already knew the basics. It's just now that I get to dive in without doing a stomach-flop. The question always was kept in the back of my mind, what happened "at the pool" on Friday, Saturday, and Sunday?

Well, well, sometimes "not knowing" is better than "knowing." This is certainly one of those times. One of my evil sisters, Ruth, told me the reason the pool was vacant of people but still full of water, was because it had no filter. On Thursdays, the water had began turning a brownish green. By Saturday, it was downright ugly from human gunk.

So, the routine was this: On Saturdays, the maintainence guys would scrub the sides with long wooden brooms to get all the gunk loose, and then that night, they would open all the drains and ALL of the water would be emptied from the pool. I have been there when it was completely empty. Walking on the bottom toward the deep end was a treasure hunt. I can't tell how many pennies, and nickels, and a few quarters I found. My pockets would get full. I didn't do that very often because the secret was out, and the crowds flocked. But still, my Daddy would get a big laugh of my bulging pockets when I got home on my bike.

Late on Saturdays, the guys were back cleaning the bottom of the pool. And at about midnight, the cleaning would be complete, and then the fun began. They would open all the incoming valves, and the fresh water would really pour in. Those filling pumps would run all night and all day Sunday. By Monday morning, like BAM, a new, clean pool had been created.

Now, here comes the Civil Rights Act of 1964 comes into play. It gave black people full access to every public place. That was no not welcomed by everyone.

In the Spring of 1965, I remember the backlash too well. "Colored", "Black", whatever, would come to the pool, but never alone. They would always come in carloads, for their own protection. The Police were there, but I am not too confident of their entire purpose. This was a huge cultural mind-shift.

The pool did not survive the summer.

City officials closed the pool, filled it fill of dirt and planted a beautiful garden of flowers, bushes, and small trees. The reason for the closing? They said, "The pool was very old, and it would be too costly to resurface it, and put in a new filtering system."

In reality, I think most whites supported the Act of equality with Blacks, but swiming with the Blacks was over the top, over their limit. So, the easiest way to not look at something is to look at something else. And that's exactly what happened. Nearby, there were tennis courts built. That softened the blow about the pool because not many local colored people played tennis.

Sometimes, there's irony within irony. Here it is. The old pool was in a city park, a highly visible place, and very close to town.

Two years later, in 1967, increased demand for a public pool findly overwhelmed the city officials. They decided to build a brand new public swimming pool. But "where" would it be built?

It was decided that, "in the public interest," it would be built away from downtown. That's one thing they got right.

The new pool was built in a part of town that shocked most everybody I knew. It was located in an area outside of town, and most of the neighborhood was colored.

The desired result was "equality". In reality, none of my friends could possibly ride our bikes there. It was simply too hard to get to.

The other reality was really something. Only blacks went to that pool.

The complicated gets even more complicated.

A "private" Country Club was built. It had a nice pool and a golf course. One had to be "invited" to be a part of it. And there was a fee to go along with that.

Issue resolved.

Really?

###Author's present day comments: 1) The lack of gratitude is a really bad thing, 2) I must "read" people accurately, without judgment, 3) motives can be either good or bad, but not at the same time, 4) Racism is a curable disease, 5) You DO with what you have.

Chapter 23
A Fishy Tale
Age 18, looking back to age 12 and also at present day at 18.

It's Springtime in Mississippi, and that means life is springing up everywhere. In Springtime, I have three favorite plants which really make me smile. First, I like the Lily, of all plants. They are everywhere, and my Mama loves to plant the bulbs early and watch them bloom. At Easter, the Lilies are everywhere at Church. My second favorite is only found in the woods. It's the Dogwood Tree. They are absolutely spectacular. They have a bloom that compares to nothing else. All the Dogwoods don't bloom. It's either the male or the female. I forget which one. The other one that I especially like is the Wisteria plant down at the city park where there used to be a swimming pool. The Wisteria plant is still there. It is so old. The roots are amazing to look at. They must be ancient. Whoever planted them years ago took great care. There are two long rows, about 30 feet in length, and they form a canopy over the top. No light penetrates through the top because it's so thick at the top. And the blooms are a deep purple. Their blooms will last until it gets really hot in the Summertime.

Today is Saturday, and so things around my house are a little slow. That's a good thing. I have had a tough week in school. We started baseball practice this week. I am excited about it, but I find that I am out of practice. I really need to improve my batting average. Hitting is not really one of the things I do best. My strongest point in baseball is fielding in right field. I have a strong throwing arm, and that really helps sometimes. I have good memories of throwing the ball toward the catcher at home base to prevent the runners from 3rd base reaching home base. That makes me laugh.

Later today, Mama and a few of her "cultural" friends from the Culture Club are going to Columbus, which is about 20 miles away. They plan to attend the annual "Pilgrimage" that happens in towns around Mississippi that were part of the Civil War. There's a big one in Columbus, and even a bigger one in Natchez. It's pretty nuts to me. Lots of people get dressed up in clothes from that period and parade around. I have been to one, and got a tour of an antebellum home in Columbus that served as a hospital for the Confederate Soldiers that got wounded in some way. That was cool to learn. Another big antebellum home nearby is Waverly Mansion. It's a huge mansion, 3 stories high. It's almost on the banks of the Tombigbee River.

I am out on the back patio playing around with my dog, Fella. I have already finished breakfast, and I brought a piece of bacon for him to enjoy. My Mama serves us sausage in the Winter and bacon in the Summertime. Go figure. I surely don't get it. Anyway, Fella chows down and makes short work for that bacon.

Daddy comes out and joins me. He has just finished his own breakfast and will go "do rounds" in a little bit. That means he will go check on the patients he has admitted into the hospital and see how they are doing. He mentions how beautifully Mama has arranged the blooming flowers, and I agree. He then hits me with a question that throws me off guard. He says, "Want to go deep sea fishing?"

I say, "Sure, when?" He responds, "Early Summer, down in Destin, Florida, where the King Mackerel will be running." "Count me in!" I say. I will look forward to that. The reason the question threw me off guard is because I thought he wanted to accompany me to go fishing for bream locally. I was scared of that. He is the most uncoordinated freshwater fisherman I have ever seen. As good of a surgeon he is, he is that bad as a fisherman. Yes, I want to be with him, but not on a pond. I might end up with him having to pull out a badly thrown lure out of my head. But in deep sea fishing, he knows what he is doing and enjoys it a lot, but just does not take the time to go very often. So I am looking forward to this trip.

However, I have some bad memories of deep sea fishing with him. My first trip to fish with him was when I was 12. He took me on my first deep sea fishing trip, down in Destin, FL, about a 5 hour drive from here. We left on a Friday at noon. Mama had packed my bag, thank goodness.

Boy, did I not know what I was in for. The drive down to Destin was pretty fun, because we went in his 1965 Mustang. That is still a really cool car.

It has bucket seats and I remember sleeping a good way of the trip. He woke me up as we were nearing the coast, because he knew I would enjoy the scenery. And I did. We first reached the Alabama coast and then got on a highway toward Destin. We don't fish the Mississippi coast because it has a big reef that gets in the way. In Destin, we don't have to go out so far. We got to Destin just in time for Supper. His favorite place to eat is at Captain Dave's. We checked into the motel and then went to the restaurant, which is right on the coast. He ordered his favorite, highly seasoned red snapper, which had been caught earlier in the day. I ordered my favorite, fried shrimp. We had all the trimmings and were stuffed. Daddy then went to Captain Dave, who owns the restaurant, and asked him how the fishing was. Dave said it had been really good. Daddy got a kick out of that.

We left the restaurant and went walking along the walkway where all the fishing boats were coming in with their booty for the day. Some had caught snapper, some had caught mackerel, and there was on that had caught a sail fish, and every body was taking pictures. It was smelly because there were guys a little older than I was then cleaning the fish. The sea gulls were close by picking up the left overs. It was a cool experience. We arrived to our place where the boat was that we were going on the next morning. It looked pretty big to me. Daddy spoke with the skipper and confirmed us being there. The skipper said there were going to be 2 other people to join us, so that meant 4 fishing and the skipper and the help-mate. He told us to be there at 6 am.

Daddy told me back at the motel that we would be going out about 25 miles away from the shore to fish. At the time, that didn't bother me.

We went to bed early anticipating the next day. We got up at 5:15 and got ourselves going. Both of us had on long sleeved shirts to protect us from the sun. Daddy brought his big hat, which was one of the biggest embarrassing moments of the trip. It's so big you can't get near him. He likes it though. I just wore my baseball cap and was satisfied.

We walk to the boat and arrived a little before 6. We met the other 2 fishermen, a man and his brother from Birmingham, AL. I was the only youngster. The captain started the motors and we leave. It didn't take long for us to get away from the harbor. The land is getting harder to see. And then then most embarrassing moment is history happened.

My Daddy actually pulled out a rope that he had in his pocket. He tied one end of the rope around my waist and then tied the other end around his own waist. I was mortified. The skipper, the help-mate, and the other 2 fishermen all smiled but I know they were really laughing on the inside. I was so embarrassed. There were so many bad things about that. First, did my Daddy think that I was about to jump overboard? OK, and then, the biggest of all. I swim like a fish. My Daddy does not know how to swim. My biggest problem was HIM falling over board! I would be doomed! I would die instantly!

And then, to make matters worse, the waves pick up and the boat is moving around. Daddy gave me some medicine earlier to help with seasickness, but it did not phase me. I felt woozy, I felt dizzy, and then came the nausea. I then rushed over to the side of the boat and started losing everything that I eaten in the last 3 days. That fried shrimp did not taste nearly as good coming up as it did going down! I felt awful.

The skipper then yelled from his perch above us where he was steering the boat. "They're here!", he yelled. Everybody got busy fishing. The help-mate got all the bait on everybody's line and threw it out. But not me. I was still on the side heaving up the contents of my feet!

My dad gave me some gum to chew for the bad taste, and then gave me some more medicine. That did help. After about 20 minutes, I was able to function semi-normally.

We caught a bunch of king mackerel. Dozens. They weighed about 20 pounds each. My Daddy told me I looked pale, but I really did feel better. The help-mate gave me a Coke. That tasted good. I was taking a break from fishing and looked back to what I thought was land. Nothing but sea. Nothing. The more I thought about it, this boat did look like the one from "Gilligan's Island". But I didn't see anybody on that boat as pretty as Mary Ann on that show. My Daddy had to do some reassuring very quickly. It was a good trip, just there had to be an initiation period, and I certainly got it.

Back to the present. Daddy and I leave for Destin this coming Friday and today is Tuesday. I already am preparing. Since I will be driving this time, I have already plotted the route, and estimated the mileage. This is going to be really fun. We have invited a friend to go with us. His name is Josh, and he will bring his two sons. Both of them are younger than me. I sure hope they don't get as sick as I did. They will take their car because they are visiting relatives on the way back.

Friday is finally here. Today is the day. While Daddy is finishing up things at his office, I am having the oil changed and putting gasoline in the car. We will be traveling in the same car as before, the Mustang. That's a fun car to drive. It's too easy to over the speed limit. Daddy gets home around 11:30 and he's already packed. So it won't be long. I have the route planned. Daddy likes for me to be his chauffeur. That's not all bad at all.

Now we are on our way. We will make our way through eastern Mississippi, then wind our way southeast through Alabama, then hit the Florida state line at Florala. I wonder why they named it that. Daddy and I are just talking and talking. When we get into mid-Alabama, Daddy decides to take a nap. Fine with me. I turn the radio on low, and listen to some good music.

When we get to Tuscaloosa, I turn southeast on an unfamiliar highway. Daddy is still asleep so I will just keep on my route. The good music helps the miles go by faster. I really like the Beatles. They put out some really good music. Paul McCartney is my favorite. He seems to be the most talented of them all.

When we get near Montgomery, AL, I wake Daddy up and tell him we need to get gas and take a potty break. After filling up and getting some cold drinks, we take a more rural route on Alabama state highways instead of the Interstate. These roads are not as well kept, but the scenery is interesting as we head south. The pine trees are different in these parts. There are lots of soybeans fields around here. The soil must be a little different, too. Daddy starts talking about his own dad. I love to hear those stories. He sounds like he was a real character, mild mannerisms and very confident. Daddy tells me how he learned when to talk and when to shut up. "Pop" is what all 4 boys called him. Daddy was the 2nd oldest. They named him Burnell. Pop was a Doctor as well. He was educated at Memphis Medical College and graduated medical school in 1897. Daddy tells me Pop used to make house calls in a horse-drawn buggy. He would travel as far as French Camp to deliver babies. One time he took my Daddy to French Camp do help do just that, deliver a baby. They stayed 3 days. French Camp is right on the Natchez Trace Parkway. The Natchez Indians used to use this pathway to travel from Natchez, Mississippi all the way up to almost Nashville, Tennessee. While Pop was delivering the baby, he was humming the tune to "Amazing Grace". Around French Camp, there are many migrant workers looking for opportunities to pick cotton. To such was Pop delivering this baby. Pop knew these people were dirt poor, but that simply was not a factor.

After mom and baby were safe, Pop and Daddy were walking out of the tent, and the father of the baby confessed he did not have any money to pay Pop. That did not bother Pop a bit. As Pop and Daddy were walking toward the horse-draw buggy, Pop saw a ragged-clothed young girl, sitting on the dirt crying. He leaned over and asked why she was crying. The young girl said, "I have nothing to give my mother for Christmas". Pop said nothing, but reached into his right pants pocket and pulled out a $20 gold piece and gave it to her. Pop then rushed himself and Daddy to the buggy and were on their way. Daddy's mouth was hanging open in amazement and asked Pop, "Why did you do that, they could not even give you some chickens for payment!" Pop softly responded, "Boy, what is it that I owe you?" Enough said.

Daddy told me that story had great impact on him. I can clearly see why.

I tell Daddy, "Come on, there's more." He then tells me something that still today impacts him. Daddy tried to enlist in the Army at the beginning of World War 2. He was rejected because he has a condition called "lazy eye" and they did not want him. But he tried. He tells me of a local man named Joe. Joe served in the U.S. Navy in World War 2, serving in the south Pacific on a mine sweeper. They would carve a path in front of the destroyers following them. It was their responsibility to clear the way of mines for the destroyers. What a dangerous job! Daddy said Joe came home safe and sound, but different. I asked Daddy to describe the difference. He said Joe was now much more of what Daddy calls a "Patriot." Joe often writes his Congressman, and tells him how much he appreciates him. He also writes letters to national leaders offering his take on national issues. Daddy thinks that's awesome. So do I. Daddy goes on to tell me a special thing that touches his heart every time he sees Joe do it. He sometimes would see Joe walking on the sidewalk in downtown West Point, and when he would walk near a store, like a barber shop, displaying the U.S. Flag, Joe would stop, do a military turn and give a salute to the flag, do a military turn, and be on his way. As Daddy tells me of Joe, whom I know, I get chills.

We approach Florala, AL, FL. Both states claim ownership of the town. That's what make it interesting. Now we are in Florida headed toward Pensacola. Now it won't take but a couple of hours to get to Destin, our destination.

We arrive at our motel in Destin. We find that Josh and his two boys are already there. This is great. It's getting near suppertime, and we plan to go to "Captain Dave's"? Where else would we go? It's the best. We get a table for 5. Daddy orders his snapper. After thinking about it for a moment, I decide to order snapper, too. I don't want to take any unnecessary chances. We all decide not to get dessert, because we are all so full.

We then walk over to the boat we will be fishing from in the morning. We check in with the Captain. He is expecting us. He seems to have gotten a new help-mate. Daddy asks the Captain about the recent fishing, and the Captain readily assures Daddy the fishing is good! So we walk around for a bit looking at the other boats, some are from other parts, like Central America, the Bahamas, and even a big sailboat from the tiny island of Belize.

It's 5:15am on Fishing Day! I get up, wash my face, get some clothes on, brush my teeth, and then I give Daddy the bathroom. I walk over to Josh's room to make sure they are up. They are, and are almost ready to go. When I get back to the room, Daddy is laughing at himself. I know he is not a morning person, so whatever he says is not going to surprise me. He says, "The tubes of Preparation H for my hemorrhoids and the tubes of Pepsodent toothpaste looked similar to me. I accidentally put Pepsodent on my hemorrhoids." I am bent over laughing. I say, "How do they feel?" His response, "Cool and refreshed!" I am just thinking to myself, "I come from the seed of this man. I am doomed."

It's fun to see the captains helpmate gather all the things necessary before we launch. He's getting plenty of ice, water, soft drinks of all kinds. He also puts sandwiches in there since that's included in the deal. I don't see him putting any chocolate cookies in the cooler. I am now disappointed and reconsidering whether are not I want to go. I may back out—just kidding. He puts all of that into a big cooler and covers it with ice. Then there's a bigger cooler just for ice. I don't know why. Daddy has given me some anti-vomit medicine. He offers this same for Josh and the two boys. They take it.

The captain starts those two big diesel engines and just lets them warm up. There pretty noisy and smelly but I guess it won't be so bad ones we get going. I hope he has enough fuel. I know I shouldn't be worried about things like this, but they do cross my mind. I know what happed to Gilligan.

The captain calls us to get together to explain the plans for the day. He explains we will be going out about 15 to 17 miles out in the ocean and stop. The intent is to do some bait catching. This is a new twist. He explains we will be catching smaller fish first and then go out about 15 miles more and use the freshly caught fish as bait for the bigger ones out in deeper water. This is getting more groovy by the moment.

It's about 6:10 AM, and we are all on board. This is just about the same size boat as before, and there are enough seats for all of us. The captain puts the boat in reverse and pulls away from the dock. It doesn't take long for us to be in the harbor. He puts the boat in "drive" (I guess that's the right word. I think of this as a truck on water). We travel pretty slowly as we leave the harbor. Other fishing boats are nearby, and everybody waves as we go by. The captain is up in his perch chattering away with other captains. Earlier he said it's in everybody's best interest to let each other know where they're headed and especially alert each other when they start catching lots of fish. I guess there's enough gravy here so everybody can sop his biscuit, so to speak.

Out of the harbor, the captain yells for everybody to sit down. Before I take a seat, I take a quick look over the side of the boat and look straight down. I can actually see the bottom! I ask that helper how deep the water years at this point. He responds, " It's about 80 feet". I am amazed the water is so clear I can see 80 feet down. I would've guessed it's about 20 feet or so. Shows you what I know. He then goes a little faster, and then after about 10 minutes, he throws it up a notch and we're going even a bit faster. The water is relatively smooth. There are just little waves we go through so far. As we get out into the ocean, I see dolphins following us, jumping out of the water. It's very entertaining. They know if we find fish, so will they. Also following us are the seagulls. There are about six or eight of them. I guess their reasoning is about the same as the dolphins. The food chain is very evident here. I really hope the food chain stops at me today. I strongly prefer not to be someone's dinner today.

The captain yells to the helper, "It's time!" The helper quickly reaches into one of the ice coolers and grabs a bag of smaller fish that are shaped like and are about the same size as a cigar. I guess that's why the helper says to us, "We'll be using cigar fish to catch the bait." I'm really glad I didn't open my mouth.

The bait for the small fish is being cast out so that the small fish can be used as bait fish later today. That process still astounds me anyway. We began pulling in the smaller fish right away. I had never done this part before. These fish are very brightly colored, and are really beautiful. We are fishing in about 100 feet of water, but I can't see the bottom anymore. All of us have our lines jiggling, and then about 20 minutes later, we catch more baitfish than we could possibly use for today. It really reminds me of the way that Paul and I run into a school of bream at home and bring in the limit in just about the same amount of time it has taken us to catch these. I say again, these are really brightly colored fish. They are muck more colorful than what I've ever seen. Some of them are bright yellow with streaks of black. After our reels are pulled in, we head out to deeper water and are hopeful to run into some good fishing. Like before, we will be fishing mainly for mackerel, which was caught by bait.

It's about 11:00 AM, and the Captain tells us we're getting close. The helper uses bigger fishing gear for this, since we are preparing to catch bigger fish. The rods and reels are like what I've seen before. I remember that last time vividly. I don't think I've eaten fried shrimp since then.

The helper has all of us ready to go. The Captain says, "Throw them out!" Everyone is excited. This is the moment we have been looking forward to for months. I lean over and tell my Daddy how thankful I am the anti-vomit medicine worked this time!

After about 10 minutes, we get our first strike, and it happens to be Daddy's line. He is laughing and reeling at the same time. Then the fish dives deep, making the reel scream as the line goes out. Daddy lets him dive, and then starts reeling in again. After about three times of the out-and-in process, the fish is tired and the helper helps Daddy bring him in. It's a King Mackeral! That's what we've been waiting on! Not long after that, all five of us have caught at least two. We know that five is the limit per pole, so we still have a lot of fishing to do. The Captain is smiling and is calling other boats and telling them we have found a good spot. About 15 minutes later, we start to see boats coming our way, but they stay their distance, not getting too close. About 20 minutes has now passed, and everybody on the boat has got their limit of Mackeral but me, so it's just me, and the ocean. After 10 to 12 minutes more of slow trolling, I get a strike, but it's not like all the rest. It's like a whale has my line and I have absolutely no control over it whatsoever. The reel is screaming as the line goes out and sounds like six cars all going 100 miles per hour and suddenly hit their breaks at the same time. It's that type of velosity. I have never felt anything this strong. The helper says to me, "That's no Mackeral!", and I try my best to reel him in some. With all my might, I pull the line in, with SOME success. Then he suddenly goes deep again. I feel him now not swiming so hard, so I reel in really hard. I bring in about 75 feet of line, and he doesn't like that at all! He immediately goes deep just like before. I don't think he's tired at all! This procedure goes on for over an hour! I have to give the reel to both Daddy and Josh at different times to give me some relief. WOW! I am sweating bullets! Josh gives the reel back to me after I have had time to drink a Coke. I am back at the helm, ready for more. This time, I am in control. Thank Goodness Daddy and Josh have worn this monster out! He does run deep again, but it's not like before. Each time now, I am making progress bringing him closer to the surface. The helper is constantly at the side with a gaft ready for anything I bring close enough. I give a really strong pull and then I hear the helper yell to the Captain, "Captain, bring your gun, he's got a shark!"

I thought to myself, "I've got a WHAT?!" The helper says for me to keep reeling him in as best I can. Meanwhile, the Captain has stopped the trolling engines, locked the wheel, and puts it in neutral. He is now at my side with a .45 revolver. Right now, I would rather be assisting my Daddy deliver a baby.

Why to these strange things keep happening to me? Everybody else is happy catching Mackeral, but me, NO! I have to catch a man-eating shark!

The Captain tells the helper to move away, and then he tells me to keep reeling. At this point, I will argue with no one. He then takes aim as I continue reeling. I bring the shark close enough for the Captain to shoot. BANG! BANG! BANG! He shoots him 3 times! My ears are ringing because he's standing right next to me!

Now I don't feel any resistance at all. I can certainly understand why. Everybody but ME is at the side wanting to see what this thing is!

The Captain turns to me and yells, "You just caught yourself a huge Hammerhead Shark!" I think to myself, "Paul will never again say he can out-fish me!" It takes both the Captain and the helper, and with Josh's help, to drag this shark into the boat!

The shark falls into the boat, really, really dead. I don't feel too far from it myself.

This is, by far, the ugliest creature on God's green Earth that I have ever seen. I used to think my sister Maggie was the ugliest thing when she 1st got out of bed. But, no, no, not anymore. She is a knock-down drag-out beauty queen compared to this creature. I mean, the eyes on either side of its head would definitely scare a ghost!

The Captain says, "It's time to go home." Nobody, I mean nobody, disagrees. Daddy tells me when the Captain came down with his gun in hand, all the boats around came closer to see the spectacle.

The helper gives us all soft drinks and we head back. Somehow, I don't understand why, it just feels like it takes a shorter time to get back to harbor than it did to get out there. Must be my imagination.

The Captain has radioed ahead and a crowd of people have gathered to see the prize! I am now a local celebrity! I can get used to this very quickly!

As the Captain tells the helper on-shore, "Hoist him up!" They put a hook in his gill and lift him high, over the side of the boat and insert him on the scales. OH, MY STARS!

This shark weighs 212 pounds! Now, it's no wonder that the Captain wanted to shoot it. This was one bad puppy! And I caught it!

OK, whew! Everybody is taking pictures and the helpers are cleaning the Mackeral. They are sliced into filets, put into plastic bags, and then covered with Dry Ice. That way, they will stay frozen until we get home. This is going to be some good eating for the months ahead.

Like my favorite baseball player, Yogi Berra says, "It ain't bragging if you've done it!"

Well, I dun done it. Hee hee.

####Author's present day reflection: 1) Keep reminding myself that my past is not my future, 2) Road trips are loads of fun, 3) Powerful lessons are to be remembered, 4) It is not a good thing to confuse "Preparation H" for toothpaste, 5) When you have a "big one", reel him in, 6) Bragging is only permissible when one has done the feat multiple times.